SACRED BLOODLINES

THE EARTH GRID SERIES BOOK 2

S.A. BECK

This is a work of fiction. Names, characters, organizations, places, events, and incidents are either products of the author's imagination or are used fictitiously.

SACRED BLOODLINES

Copyright © 2020 by S.A. Beck

ISBN: 978-1-987859-75-1

www.sabeckbooks.com

DELLA MARSHAL WAS NOT HAVING a good summer.

She had nearly been killed by her graduate advisor and had been cursed by a millionaire and investigated by the police and had the most interesting archaeological investigation of her career cancelled.

Now she was scrambling to find a new advisor at the Oxford University Department of Archaeology while most of the faculty were away on excavations in far-flung corners of the world, and at the same time desperately trying to convince herself that the strange paranormal events that had led to her advisor's death were somehow her imagination. Or hypnotism. Or hallucinations. Or someone slipping acid into her beer for several days in a row. Because to accept what she had seen as the truth would break her hold on reality. She was too sensitive for this sort of thing. Even socializing with friendly people brought a lot of strain. Fighting for her life had made her hole up in her flat, shaken and afraid, for a couple of weeks with no company except her books.

Oh, and her cute boyfriend had gone gay on her. That had been great for her self-esteem. Just great.

And now she was outside a noisy London pub, witnessing a kidnapping.

The day had started with an invitation to go down to the Bloomsbury Book Fair, held every couple of months in a hotel on Russell Square, close to the British Museum.

Lucas Lancaster—carpenter, sheep farmer, and self-proclaimed wizard—had invited her to join him there. At first she had been tempted to say no. He'd saved her life, and she had saved his, during the whole mess with her advisor's cult, but Della still felt uncomfortable around him. He was a weirdness magnet, and Della had had quite enough weirdness for one summer. Or lifetime.

Eventually she had relented, partly because she was feeling bored up at Oxford with no project to do and partly because the Bloomsbury Book Fair was famous as one of the best places to find rare volumes on every subject imaginable.

And partly, although she wouldn't admit this to herself, Lucas was great company. And cute. And not gay.

At least she didn't think so. He was cocooned in such a shell of strangeness and solitude that it was hard to figure out anything about him.

So they took the bus down to London together and ended up at the Hotel Russell, an ornate Victorian building of red brick overlooking a green square where kids played in a fountain and couples lounged on the grass, eating sandwiches and enjoying a lovely British summer day.

But who needs sun and grass and fountains when you can have an exhibition room filled with book dealers?

Della gasped when they entered. There must have been a couple of hundred dealers here, each with their own large table piled high with books. They walked down the aisles, shouldering through the crowd of studious-looking men and women perusing the displays of rare volumes. Some dealers had a variety of books, but most specialized in a particular subject. She passed one table filled with books on polar exploration, including a signed first edition of *The South Pole: An Account of the Norwegian Expedition in the* Fram, *1910–12* by Roald Amundsen, leader of the first expedition to the South Pole. She'd always thrilled to the exploits of the early explorers.

"This might be interesting," she said.

"I'd suggest looking at the price," Lucas said with a smile.

She did, shuddered, and put it back.

"Don't worry," Lucas said. "There are books for all budgets here. Try to stay away from signed first editions, and you'll be on safer ground."

They went on, looking through tables of French novels and books on royalty, Renaissance history, and Soviet propaganda. One table stopped them short. Instead of books, it displayed official documents, everything from telegrams sent to the families of men who had died on the Western Front to court rulings from the time of King George III. Pride of place went to a glass case that held a land deed with the seal of Henry VIII. Both of them stared.

"There's no price tag," Lucas said.

"If you have to ask, you can't afford it."

"You're learning."

They smiled at each other and continued. Della found a table with archaeological volumes and started digging. Lucas left her after a while, saying he was going to find some "specialist" dealers he knew personally. Della suspected that meant occult book dealers and gladly let him go. When he was delving into the occult was the only time he wasn't good company.

She finally decided on two purchases—an out-of-print volume from 1928 titled *Medieval German Kingdoms* and the 1836 issue of *Archaeologia or Miscellaneous Tracts Relating to Antiquity*, published by the Royal Society of Antiquaries of London. Her undergraduate library back in the States had an entire run, and she had loved looking through the beginnings of her science and the lovely engravings that illustrated the articles. She had always wanted a copy of her own, and now she had one. It had burst her budget, but she felt she deserved some comfort books. When depressed, Della consumed books the way some women consumed chocolate ice cream.

After Della said goodbye to the man running the stall, an elderly Yorkshireman who had happily chatted to her about archaeology as she looked at his stock, she went to find Lucas. He was talking to the strangest-looking man she had ever seen.

The man was a dealer with a table that, not

surprisingly, displayed various occult volumes. He was as thin as a rake, nearly seven feet tall, with a bony face that had sunken cheeks, wild blue eyes, and a messy shock of brown hair in desperate need of a trim. As Della approached, he was in animated conversation with her friend, his overly large hands moving constantly to emphasize his points.

"And in the Raising Ceremony of the Five Keys, we learned that... oh, hello."

The book dealer turned to her, and Della immediately found herself under inspection. Not the usual quick glance up and down guys made before kinda-sorta making eye contact but a riveting stare right into Della's eyes that made her social anxiety disorder go into overdrive. She looked away.

Lucas gestured to the book dealer.

"Della, I'd like you to meet Montague James."

"Not *the* Montague James," the book dealer said and then cackled so loudly that he made Della jump.

Lucas laughed, too, although in a much more normal way.

"You never get tired of that joke, do you, Montague?"

Della decided not to reveal that she had no idea who Montague James was.

Montague extended a bony, oversized hand. He

was still staring at her eyes, trying to make eye contact.

"Pleased to meet you, Della. I'm always proud to meet a warrior." His grip was surprisingly firm.

"I beg your pardon?"

Montague leaned forward and said in a conspiratorial whisper, "Lucas told me everything."

Della rounded on her friend. "You what?"

"Allies, Della. Allies. Just because we stopped one manifestation of evil doesn't mean we won't have to face more."

Della rolled her eyes. Soon the conversation shifted back to occult matters, and Della tuned out. She rummaged through the books on display, some quite old and expensive. Many looked self-published. Why would anyone believe this stuff?

Because a lot of this stuff is real, a part of her mind told her. She shoved that thought firmly back in the gutter where it belonged.

She tuned back in when the two men turned to her.

"Would you be up for a pint at a historic pub this evening?" Lucas asked.

Della hesitated. "Oh, well, I do have some work to do in Oxford."

Lucas held up a finger. "I happen to know that

you do not. I'm indirectly responsible for getting you fired, remember? Come on. Montague will be there, and you'll get to meet my old friend Autumn."

"A member of the British royal family," Montague added.

"Really?" Della asked. If one word could have carried all the cynicism and sarcasm in the world, it would have been that one. Della felt like she was thirteen again.

"Della is a compulsive disbeliever," Lucas explained to his weird friend.

"Opposites attract," Montague said.

Della groaned inwardly. This was going to be a long day. She just knew it.

Four hours later, after more book buying and a visit to the British Museum, where Lucas showed a remarkable knowledge of ancient history, Della found herself in a pub in the City, which was what Londoners called the financial heart of London.

The pub was called the Postern. A plaque on the front of the dark-wooden-frame building explained that the pub stood atop a small gate in the old city walls. Unlike a lot of canned pub "history" that you found on menus and beer mats, Della thought this might actually be true. A short trace of the old wall, now only waist high, stood farther down the road, railed off from the hurrying businessmen and honking traffic. The building itself looked at least three hundred years old.

"Like it?" Lucas asked. "I thought it would appeal to you."

Della nodded. They entered the dim interior, which was broken up into little side rooms with a larger room at the center mostly taken up by a gleaming if somewhat battered old brass bar. They got drinks and moved to a side table where they saw Montague sitting with a woman who looked to be in her early thirties.

She was what the British called "posh"—perfect hair, turned-up nose, a tan that told of a recent holiday in the Maldives or the south of France, expensive jewelry, a dainty Rolex watch, and a brilliant diamond necklace. She looked out of place, almost comical next to Montague with his faded jacket of green tweed and his too-short corduroy pants.

But they appeared to be the best of friends, chatting away eagerly and not even noticing Lucas and Della until they were actually sitting down at the table.

The woman rose to air-kiss Lucas near both of his cheeks and then took Della by the hand.

"You must be Lucas's little archaeologist. How nice to meet you. I'm Autumn Birgit Saxe-Coburg."

"Nice to meet you too," Della said in a flat voice.

Autumn turned to Lucas, and Della got the distinct impression that she had just been put permanently out of the conversation.

"Lucas! Good news. I was just telling Montague that my lawsuit is going forward."

"Oh, that's excellent." Lucas turned to Della. "Autumn is the love child of George Saxe-Coburg, Duke of Anhalt." When Della didn't reply, he explained. "The cousin of the queen."

Then Della remembered. The royal family came from Germany back in the nineteenth century because of some royal politics she had never bothered to look up. Their original family name had been Saxe-Coburg. They had changed it during the First World War because the army found it embarrassing to be fighting the Germans under orders from a king with a German name. Some of the German branch of the family had kept their original name.

But this snotty rich woman wasn't in the royal line. Surely not. She wouldn't keep this kind of company.

Autumn waved a hand in front of Lucas's face.

"Lucas, you're not *listening*. My barrister says we have an even chance of gaining recognition."

She went on to relate a complex tangle of legal arguments. Lucas tried to keep Della in the conversation, but Autumn would always get impatient and hog all his time. When Della started a side conversation with Montague, Autumn did the same with the book dealer. So Della tuned out. Della had a lot of experience in tuning out. Most people were annoying, and this woman was especially so. Wandering off into her own thoughts brought welcome respite. She sipped her pint and looked around at the old interior of the pub, with its prints of fox hunts and crumbling medieval castles. She felt the heavy bulk the rare books she had bought made in her bag. She checked her phone to find that no one had texted her. She wondered if she could make some excuse and leave early, but Lucas would try to get her to stay.

Oh well, at least most of the day had been fun. Lucas was good company when he wasn't acting like a lunatic. This Montague fellow didn't seem all bad either. While he scored a bit too high in the weirdo department, he seemed nice enough, and it wasn't like Della was qualified to judge people on their social skills.

But Autumn? A fake if there ever was one. A shallow, spoiled rich girl making up stories about herself in a desperate bid to seem interesting. She couldn't believe two intelligent men like Lucas and Montague had fallen for her story.

At last, Autumn said the thing that Della most wanted to hear. She glanced at her expensive watch and remarked, "Oh my, look at the time. I really must be going, darlings. I have a dinner appointment with the Marquis of Lucerne. Adorable little man and such good taste in wines."

"We'll walk you out," Lucas said. "It's time to make a move anyway. Della, shall we get one for the road at another pub?"

"Sure." She was happy to go along with anything now that this superficial bore fest was over.

They stepped out into the night. With England's long summer, it was still soft twilight at nine. A van with the logo of some plumbing company stood outside, the back doors open. A couple of burly men with caps low over their eyes leaned against it, smoking cigarettes. They eyed Autumn. Della tensed. She hated it when men stared at her. It made her feel awkward. But she hated men ignoring her in favor of another woman even more.

You really need to learn how to relax, she chided herself.

The four of them stood on the sidewalk.

"You sure you can't come for another pint?" Montague asked. Della's heart sank.

"No, darling, I really must go. Oh, and here's a cab just coming along now. Ta-da!"

She turned to wave to the cab.

And then the men next to the plumbers' van grabbed her.

2

IT HAPPENED SO FAST that Lucas didn't have time to react. The two men grabbed Autumn by the arms, one on each side, and hauled her to the back of the van, tossing her in just as she let out her first scream. One leaped into the back with her while the other turned to face Lucas, who had started after them. The man let loose with a brutal right hook that took Lucas off his feet and laid him out on the pavement.

He must have blanked out for a second, because the next thing he knew, Della was next to him, swinging her bag of books at his attacker. She clocked him right on the side of the head, making him stagger back.

But not for long. The man snarled and surged forward, swinging his meaty fists.

He wouldn't hit a woman, would he? Lucas thought as he tried and failed to rise.

Of course he would, you bloody idiot. He just kidnapped one, didn't he?

Della obviously realized the same thing, because she nimbly retreated, swinging her heavy bag of books again. The man batted it away angrily and wound up for a punch.

Lucas grabbed him by a foot and tugged, putting him momentarily off balance.

Della hit him with the books again. The man shrugged it off, kicked Lucas in the ribs, and then gave Montague a one-two punch to the stomach as he dove into the fight.

His friend let out a grunt and ended up on his knees beside Lucas.

A call from the van made their attacker back off. He jumped in the back of the van and slammed the door, cutting off the sound of Autumn's screams.

The van revved up and shot down the street, narrowly missing a pedestrian who had to scramble out of the way.

Lucas struggled to sit up, his nose bleeding

freely. Della and Montague managed to get him to his feet as a crowd gathered.

"Call the police!" Montague shouted. "A woman has been kidnapped."

"I'll do it," Della said, pulling out her phone and calling 999. "I got the license number."

"It won't be real," Lucas groaned. His words came out sounding stuffy thanks to the blood flowing freely from both nostrils. "The van is stolen, or at least the plates are."

Montague shook his head and looked anxiously down the road. "I warned her about this. I told her to be careful."

"What's going on? What do you mean?" Della asked.

Lucas looked around at the staring crowd and felt a flush of embarrassment at being knocked down in front of so many people. "Not here. I'll explain later. First we must speak with the police."

"Fat lot of good they'll do," Montague grumbled.

Della got the emergency services on her phone, and within five minutes, a patrol car and an ambulance were at the scene. They told their story to the police, who put in a call to dispatch, giving the description of the van and the license number Della had spotted.

"Can you remember anything else about the men?" the officer asked.

They had given only a vague description.

"Sorry. We weren't paying much attention. It all happened so fast," Lucas said. He was sitting in the back of the ambulance as a medic stuffed cotton up his nose.

The officer glanced up. "At least there will be CCTV footage."

England had a profusion of security cameras on public streets, London having the most of all.

"You won't see their faces," Montague said. "They had caps on and kept their heads bowed."

Lucas nodded. He had forgotten that. Considering how grainy the images of crimes always were on the nightly news, he wondered if that precaution had even been necessary.

"Do you know any reason why someone might want to kidnap your friend?" the officer asked.

Lucas and Montague exchanged glances.

"None at all," Montague said.

The police took their information and were soon gone. The woman who had treated Lucas assured him that his nose was not broken, and the ambulance left as well.

Lucas and his two mismatched friends stood on the pavement, for a moment at a loss.

"Now what?" Montague asked.

Lucas's mind was a whirl. "I don't know. Let's sit down and figure this out."

Della put a hand on his arm. It felt reassuring, even if Della was as powerless as he was. "I'm so sorry for your friend. We should go back to Oxford so you can lie down. I'm sure the police will find them. They got CCTV and the license plate number and—"

"The police won't find her at all," Lucas said with sudden conviction. "Within an hour or so, they'll stop looking."

Della stared at him in wonder. "What are you talking about?"

He glanced at Montague. His old friend knew exactly what he was talking about. The book dealer gave him a look that seemed to say, *Can she be trusted?* He gave a little nod as an answer.

"Let's go get another pint and talk this through."

He led them down the street toward another pub he knew. He didn't want to go back into the Postern. Too many people would come over, wanting him to relate what they'd already seen. The average man and woman on the street could be highly annoying. That was one thing that he and Della agreed on.

It was a Sunday evening, so most pubs weren't that busy. He picked a quiet one, but the landlord turned them out.

"We don't want any troublemakers here," he said, gesturing at Lucas's bloody shirt.

"He's not a troublemaker," Della said. "His friend got—"

"Never mind. Let's go," Lucas said.

Montague lent him his green tweed jacket. It was old and hideous and far too big for him, but with the front buttoned up, he at least didn't look like he'd just come out the loser in a cage fight.

They found a quiet pub, and Lucas moved over to an isolated table in a far corner while Montague and Della distracted the barmen. When they had settled down to drinks, Lucas began.

"Della, I saw how you reacted to Autumn. That's understandable, but she really is what she says she is. I suspect that's why she was kidnapped."

Della cocked her head. "She really is related to the queen? How do you know?"

Lucas let out a breath of relief. Getting Della to believe anything the least out of the ordinary was harder than getting a loan out from a bank. Seeing poor Autumn kidnapped in the middle of a busy street probably helped with that.

"I met her first," Montague said. "She was looking for certain works on the royal houses of Europe. I sell rare volumes on the genealogies of lesser-known branches of royal families, both those that exist now and those that are extinct."

"I thought you sold occult books."

"There's a great deal of connection between the two. We'll get into that in a moment. She told me her story about being a rejected illegitimate member of the British royal family. I must admit I didn't believe her at first. One meets all sorts of crackpots in this business."

"You don't say."

Lucas sighed and took a long pull from his pint. They were losing her already.

Montague didn't seem to notice. "Oh yes, indeed. But then she started telling me more, and she knew so much. And she showed me documents."

"Documents? What sort of documents?"

"Letters, family photos, that sort of thing. The problem was, the royals didn't want to recognize her. She was the product of an illicit affair, you see, and that could be very damaging to the palace."

"But didn't you say this guy, her father, was just

some cousin of theirs still living in Germany? Why would it matter what he did?"

Lucas leaned forward. "The British royal family is in a delicate moment. Their popularity is on the wane. Not only do most of the younger generation not give a fig about who's on the throne, but many of the more radical element on both the left and the right don't like the idea of royalty at all. And then there's the immigrant population. They weren't born under the House of Windsor and don't feel any great loyalty for it, and they bring up their children the same way."

"Now you're talking like Whitaker."

Lucas frowned. "I most certainly am not. I'm merely stating facts. Most of the immigrant population has no emotional connection to the royal family, and why should they? Saying that doesn't make me a white supremacist."

Della put up a calming hand. "You're right. That was unfair. Go on."

"So anyway, the last thing the palace needs is some big scandal. Autumn has tried to get the attention of the press, but they thought she was a loon. I'm sure there were a few phone calls from the palace and chats in the right gentlemen's clubs. At that level, they all know each other, after all. Most are old school chums."

"But I thought you said Autumn had proof."

"Nothing the papers could use as proof for the general public," Montague said. "Letters can be faked. Old photographs are open to interpretation. I wouldn't have believed any of that myself if it were not for the real proof she showed."

"And what was that?" Della asked.

Here we go. Lucas took another long pull from his pint to steady himself. He'd let Montague explain it. Let him take the cutting looks and disparaging remarks. He hated it when Della did that to him.

"There are certain rituals that can only be performed by someone with royal blood," Montague began.

Yep, there was that cutting look. The disparaging remarks would be coming along shortly.

"So Autumn is some sort of queen of the witches?" Della asked.

Oh yes, right on cue. Although considering how shabbily Autumn had treated her, one couldn't really blame Della for that little jibe.

Montague appeared oblivious. While he was a brilliant occultist, he was oblivious about a great many things.

"Not exactly a queen, and she didn't practice Wicca. She did try out some rituals under my direction, however, as a test. She knows a bit about the occult, as it relates to her status, and much of occult lore and secret royal history is closely entwined. She was not a high priestess, though. I think I might be forgiven if I said that Autumn is a bit too—how shall I put it?—*flighty* to ascend very high in occult circles."

"I'd certainly forgive you," Della said dryly.

"Um, yes. She's a darling, as she would put it, and quite enjoyable company. Certainly easy on the eyes," Montague said with a chuckle.

"Could we get to the point?" Della asked.

"Oh yes, right. When she came to me with all this evidence, you might say I was less than convinced. So I discussed some of the more occult aspects of her lineage with her and asked her if she'd like to raise the spirit of one of her dead ancestors."

Della did not reply. Montague took that as interest. Lucas knew better.

"I decided that we should raise the shade of one of the old barons of Anhalt, one who had lived in the seventeenth century. I have some of his personal papers in my possession giving details of his work in demonology, work that was not generally known. I decided to test her by doing a summoning with her. I could raise the fellow myself, but he would only reveal his secrets to someone of his own lineage. I decided I would have Autumn ask him some questions that I already knew the answers to but were things that he would only reveal to a member of his family. That way we could make sure we had summoned the right spirit."

"You wouldn't want to find yourself talking to the wrong spirit," Della said.

Lucas groaned and took another gulp from his pint.

"Exactly. So we did the summoning easily enough. Autumn took it all as a bit of a gag, at least until the spirit appeared. She was frightened, of course, but she quickly regained her poise. She has seen much of the world and isn't easily put off. She asked the questions I'd prompted her to ask, and he answered them correctly, thus proving her to be the baron's descendant."

Della waved her hand impatiently. "What does this all have to do with her kidnapping?"

Lucas cut in. "We're not entirely sure. Autumn had mentioned before that shadowy figures followed her sometimes at night, that she thought she was being watched. She wasn't sure who and couldn't give any faces or names, but she felt they were closing in on her. At first we thought this might be the royal family pressuring her to give up her lawsuit. She'd been offered a payment for her silence, which she had refused, and after that had received a number of threatening phone calls."

"What kind of threats?" Della asked.

"Just hang-up calls. But they happened repeatedly and in the middle of the night. Twice she changed her phone number, but they would start up again that very same day."

"Did she trace the numbers?"

"Blocked. And when she asked for records from the phone company, they denied the calls had ever been made."

"But her own phone would have records of the call, even if it didn't show the number," Della said.

Lucas shook his head. "That's the funny thing. Her phone didn't record the calls either. It was like it had been hacked."

Della arched an eyebrow. "Or maybe she was making it all up to sound interesting and important?"

Lucas looked her in the eye, feeling annoyed. How much did this woman have to witness before she began to see the world as it really was?

"Did she make up her kidnapping? Did she make up that punch I got in the nose?"

Della shrugged. When she didn't reply, Lucas went on.

"Like Montague said, there are many rituals that require someone with royal blood in their veins. Many of those spells are not very nice. Autumn might be a bit flighty, as you so readily agreed, but she's a good egg. She does a lot of charity for orphans, for example. She wouldn't have agreed to perform any black magic."

"Did anyone ever ask her to?" Della asked.

"Not that we know of..." Lucas hesitated, twirling his near-empty glass between his fingers. "There's another possibility."

"What's that?"

Montague leaned forward. "Sacrifice. There are a few rituals, very rare, that involve using royal blood, either in part or in whole. Autumn might have been abducted to act not as a practitioner for a ritual but as one of its material components."

Della went pale.

Montague saw them to the bus stop. Della had been silent for the rest of the evening as he and Lucas discussed what they could do to help Autumn. They hadn't come up with much. They'd need to dig around a bit, ask their contacts in the occult field, and see if they could think of something.

Della got on the bus. Montague tugged at Lucas's sleeve to detain him. They stood aside as the other passengers filed on.

"I hope we didn't do wrong by telling your friend so much," Montague said.

Lucas sighed. "She can be trusted, but she can't be relied upon."

"How do you mean?"

"She's a skeptic through and through. I told you all about that mess with Whitaker. Despite all she saw, despite all the evidence laid in front of her, she is still trying to push it aside. It's remarkable what the human mind can ignore when it wants to."

Montague smiled. "I'm surprised she spends time with you then. Wouldn't the best way to put all that behind her be to not speak to you at all? Or perhaps she has a different motivation."

Lucas felt himself flush. "Let's focus on Autumn."

Montague nodded. "I'll get right on it. You too. And if your archaeologist friend can be of any help, get her on board as well."

"Assuming she believes a single word of it."

"Oh, I think we convinced her."

3

DELLA DIDN'T BELIEVE a word of it.

Secret royal lineages, bribes from Buckingham Palace, raising dead barons from the grave... come *on*.

It was all just more of Lucas's ridiculous occultism. And Montague was even more out there than he was. Why did such a nice guy always have to surround himself with crazy people?

And Autumn was the craziest of the lot. While Montague lacked in social graces, to put it mildly, and Lucas losing his parents had set him on the wrong path, what excuse did Autumn have? She had money, looks, style, and heaps of connections, and yet she insisted on pretending to be something more than she was.

Still, Della reflected, the fact that Autumn's

crazy fantasy of being a royal love child was false didn't matter in a way. If the kidnappers believed it, Autumn still could have been captured for her supposedly royal blood. If Della's friendship with Lucas had taught her anything, it was that there was no shortage of crazy people in England who would believe in that sort of thing.

Like Keaton Whitaker and her own advisor, Dr. Patricia Olding.

Della trembled. Just a few short weeks before, she had come very close to dying.

So maybe the kidnappers really did want to use Autumn for some arcane ritual. Anyone investigating the crime should know about all this. It might help them track her down.

Lucas and Montague should have told the police.

But who would have believed them? And it wasn't like they could offer any leads. Autumn's tales of "shadowy figures" weren't exactly helpful.

That poor woman.

Although Autumn was a snob, an insecure rich girl hogging all the attention, and maybe even a little bit unbalanced, she didn't deserve to be kidnapped.

That look of terror on her face... those screams...

Della shuddered to think about what might be happening to her.

No, she had to do the right thing and try to get the police to understand. Maybe if it came from someone rational like her, they'd accept it a bit more than if they heard it from a loon like Montague.

The officer who had interviewed them outside the Postern had given her his card. She called the number. She got a message that he was out on patrol, so she left her number and a message saying that she had some important details regarding the case.

Then she settled down to read the books she had bought the day before. Today was going to be a nesting day. Meeting new people was always stressful for her, even when they were normal and didn't get kidnapped right before her eyes.

An hour into her reading, just when the stresses of the previous day were easing into a relaxing flow of words and images from the distant past, her phone rang.

She set aside the one-hundred-fifty-year-old archaeological journal with a sigh and picked up.

"Hello, Ms. Marshal? This is PC Summerall. I'm calling about the alleged kidnapping you reported yesterday."

"Alleged kidnapping?"

"Yes, well, the case has taken a rather strange turn. We heard from Ms. Dreiser."

"Who?"

Now it was the officer's turn to sound confused. "Ms. Autumn Dreiser. Your friend?"

"Her last name is Saxe-Coburg."

"Um, no, it is not. Her legal name is Autumn Dreiser. She is known to police for harassing the palace with claims of being a poor relation. Ms. Dreiser is rather unstable and has pulled stunts like this before."

"Stunts?"

"Making dramatic bids for attention. She has rather overstepped herself this time, though. Faking a kidnapping. And that punch her associate gave Mr. Lancaster was real enough. Have you heard from her?"

"No. I only met her last night."

"Oh, I see. Then you should be aware that she is a compulsive liar and has been arrested several times for public disorder and harassing palace staff. We referred her to the NHS for psychiatric evaluation, but she refused to go. We would very much like to speak with her. She's wanted for public affray and wasting police time."

"Wait. How do you know she wasn't kidnapped?"

"She rang us. She heard that you called the

authorities, and she got in touch to say that it was a prank designed to help her case against the palace. When she realized it had become a police matter, she got frightened and decided to admit the hoax."

"How do you know it was her?"

"She called from her phone."

"It could have been someone else."

PC Summerall let out a sigh. "Ms. Marshal, this woman is very well known to the police. As I said, she has caused all sorts of trouble over the past few years, and this is very much in keeping with her previous behavior. She also sent a photo showing us she was all right."

"Could you forward that to me?"

"Gladly."

A moment later, the image came through. It was unmistakably Autumn. She stood in a different dress, next to a newspaper kiosk where today's date on the newspapers could clearly be seen. She had a bashful look on her face and was flashing the okay sign.

"Oh," Della said.

"I'm sorry you were taken in by her, Ms. Marshal. You are not the first."

"No, I'm not."

"She is still wanted for questioning. We checked her flat, but she wasn't there. When we entered, we found her wardrobe was all but cleaned out, no jewelry was in the flat, and no suitcases. We believe she has left the city or perhaps the country. Do you have any idea where she might have gone?"

"None. Have you talked to Lucas and Montague?"

"I have. They were less than cooperative."

Why doesn't that surprise me?

"I'm afraid those two bought her story," she said.

"Then they are setting themselves up for disappointment. I've spoken to the palace security team about this, and they've had a great deal of experience with this individual. She is unstable although highly convincing. No doubt she has taken more people in. Hopefully we'll soon bring her to justice and get her the help that she so obviously needs."

"Well, thanks for the call, Officer."

"Goodbye."

With a profound sense of relief, Della put down her phone, went back to her comfy sofa, and started reading her book again. Only as she did so did she realize just how much stress the events of the previous day had put her under. It wasn't only the sudden attack and Lucas's nose flowing with blood. It was the possibility of being dragged on another trip through the unknown. Lucas and Montague had seemed so certain of some grand conspiracy at work, and she could tell that they had already been planning an investigation that she would have inevitably been roped into.

But Autumn had turned out to be a fraud. Now maybe Lucas would give some thought to all the other nonsense he subscribed to.

Because some of that was downright dangerous. Some of that stuff led to a lot worse than a bloody nose ...

A strange ritual in a field... a pair of human eyes found in an ancient monument... something attacking her in her very own apartment...

Della put her hands over her eyes, dropping her book.

No. Something didn't attack her here. Some*one* did. First Whitaker then someone else. A human being. A murderer. Not some evil spirit like Lucas and his weird friends thought. Whitaker had spiked her drink with some sort of psychotropic drug. He had used the power of suggestion, maybe even hypnotism, to get her to believe in what they believed in.

And despite her grounding in science, despite her keen analytical mind, she had fallen for it.

She shouldn't be so hard on herself, Della

decided. What with her advisor turning out to be in a cult and the murders and herself nearly getting killed, who could blame her if she thought some of that might be real? She'd nearly had a mental breakdown, and then they drugged her.

Della got up, her legs unsteady, and crossed the room to put her phone on silent. She didn't want to be disturbed. She needed a long day with tea and books and no people. She still hadn't recovered from all that had happened. That wasn't her being a mental case; anyone would react like this.

Della had always been sensitive about her sensitivity. She looked upon her social anxiety disorder and poor social skills with contempt. It had taken all of high school and part of her undergraduate years to remove the term "loser" from her self-description. And no matter how good her grades or how impressive her accomplishments, it still occasionally crept in.

You need down time, she told herself. *You've been through a legit traumatic experience that would throw anyone for a loop. There's a month before term starts. Take it off. Read. Bury yourself in the library. Drink tea. Watch movies. You deserve it.*

And avoid the crazy cute guy you're kind of

attracted to even though he's a nutjob. He'll only draw you into more drama.

She read and tried to relax.

Tried and failed.

Her eyes passed over the lines without really focusing on the words. She kept turning to look at her phone on the table.

Growling, she went and made tea. Drank it. Tried to read again.

"Augh, you win!" she cried, throwing her hands in the air.

Della stomped over to her phone and checked it. There were three missed calls from Lucas. Of course there were.

She called him. He picked up on the first ring.

"Oh, hello," he said like her call was a big surprise. "My aunt and uncle were wondering if you'd like to come over for dinner tonight."

"Be honest, Lucas."

"Honest?"

"You want me to go over there so you can tell me whatever grand conspiracy theory you've cooked up about Autumn and then get me to help you investigate."

"Della..."

"She called the cops and admitted it was a hoax.

The policeman from last night said she sent you and Montague a photo of her from this morning showing she was all right. He sent it to me too. She's fine."

"You mean the photo by the kiosk? That photo actually proves she's been kidnapped."

Della rolled her eyes and groaned. "All right, tell me."

He was going to anyway, so she might as well give him permission.

"It would be better if we sat down and discussed this at length."

That's exactly what I don't want to do, Della thought. Unfortunately for her, she had never been good at speaking plainly to people who were being annoying. She was far too shy for that. She was getting better, though.

"I'm feeling very tired and overwhelmed," she said. That was true enough and not confrontational.

"Really? I seem to recall that I was the one who was punched in the nose."

"Oh my god, I didn't even ask how you were. I'm sorry."

"Not as sorry as I am. It still hurts. The bleeding is all gone, at least. If I moaned in pain once or twice, wouldn't that make you feel guilty enough to come?"

Della laughed as a way to avoid answering the question.

"How about I up the stakes?" Lucas said. "You want to relax. You're 'nesting,' as you like to say. Well, come stay the night. My uncle and aunt would love to have you, the guest bedroom is all made up, and you can help feed the sheep tomorrow morning."

"They're adorable!"

"Is that a yes?"

"Are you trying to use cute sheep, a relaxing farm, and tasty food to bribe me into joining you on some wild goose chase for a fake royal? You're unbelievable."

"If you think that's unbelievable, wait until you hear our story."

4

WHEN LUCAS GOT off the phone with Della, he did a little happy dance, immediately stopped himself, and stood there feeling embarrassed for a second. Here Autumn had gone missing, and he was getting excited about Della coming over.

He couldn't deny he had developed some feelings for her since what had happened earlier that summer, but he was realistic enough to know that she didn't share them.

It didn't matter so much. At least she'd be over here for a whole evening and the following morning.

But she will be here for work, he reminded himself. *Even if she doesn't know that yet. Focus on the important things, and don't get distracted by your own loneliness.*

Della showed up just in time for supper, as she had said she would. It nettled him a bit that she wasn't early.

She doesn't want to deal with her powers, he reminded himself. *And she's smart enough to know that you'll try to draw on them. It's amazing she's come at all.*

Lucas watched from the library as she parked her car on the gravel drive and Uncle Philip came up from the field, wearing a pair of muddy wellies and overalls. She smiled and gave him a big hug, not noticing that the portly old farmer got her jeans muddy. They walked together to the house.

He could see her look over the house with an appreciative eye. The house dated to the Tudor period, built atop the foundations of a medieval manor that was itself built atop the foundations of an Anglo-Saxon church. Little trace of those had survived except for the cellar, which he had shown Della on a previous visit and which she declared to be of medieval make. What he hadn't told her was that the Anglo-Saxons had built a church here to eradicate a prehistoric stone circle and its associated cult. Aunt Mary had told him this, and the way she had found out would not have been accepted by Della's stubbornly scientific mind.

Della also hadn't spent much time in the library in which Lucas stood. She might have been a book-worm, but she had no appreciation for one of the most extensive private collections of occult books in all of Europe.

Aunt Mary answered the door with a joyful cry, no doubt giving Della a hug as strong as Uncle Philip's.

He heard Aunt Mary chide his uncle for tracking mud into the house and his response that it added to the ambiance of the front hall. This back and forth was almost as old as the house itself. Then he heard them move through to the kitchen, where no doubt Aunt Mary had prepared one of her innumerable kettles of tea.

Still Lucas stayed in the library. He passed his hand over the aged leather spines, studying the gold lettering. Then he went over to a worn old oak table where several books on royal lines were open to complex charts of genealogies.

Yes, it was all there, just as Montague had said it would be.

The sound of happy conversation drifted through from the kitchen. Uncle Philip's raised voice called, "Lucas, your friend's here!"

Lucas cringed. He hoped Della hadn't caught

the slight ironic emphasis on the word "friend." Being around her was hard enough without his aunt and uncle playing matchmaker.

The crunch of tires on the gravel drive made Lucas sigh with relief. Finally, reinforcements had arrived.

"Be there in a minute," he called back. "The others are here."

He had asked his friend Richard Camilo to pick up Montague at the bus station. The older Afro-Caribbean man was one of the book dealer's best customers. While Richard's occult library couldn't rival Aunt Mary's, being collected as it was over several generations of witches and warlocks, it wasn't for lack of trying.

"Glad you could come, Montague," he said as he opened the door for him.

"A friend in need is a friend indeed," the book dealer said, having to duck to get through the door.

"Thank you for coming, too, Richard."

"No worries, mate. I've always wanted to meet Autumn."

"With your help, we might just be able to arrange that."

They passed through into the kitchen. Della let out a happy cry and went to hug Richard.

"So good to see you again!" she said.

"We'll have to have another party," Richard replied.

Della put on a look of mock horror. "Oh, no! It took me all the next day to recover from your last party."

"And I nearly put my back out carrying you up the stairs to your flat," Lucas grumbled. He left out the part about her trying to kiss him. He wasn't sure whether she remembered or not.

Della looked at Richard then Montague, who stood awkwardly in the doorway, and then at Lucas with a look that said, *I knew you were roping me into something.*

They all sat down at the kitchen table, having to crowd around as Uncle Philip fetched some extra chairs. Once everyone had been served some tea, Lucas cleared his throat and spoke.

"As nice as it is to have you all here for tea, we have a serious matter to attend to. You've all heard bits of it, but now that we're all together, we can catch one another up and work on a way forward. Autumn has been kidnapped."

Della opened her mouth to object. Lucas cut her off.

"Montague and I both got a message from her

saying she was all right. The police got a similar message, but we know that isn't true."

"How can you know that?" Della objected. "PC Summerall sent me the photo. She looks all right to me."

As she took out her phone and looked for the photo, Montague replied, "We agreed that if she was in trouble, she'd send us a photo where she's flashing the okay sign."

Uncle Philip turned to him and frowned. "Isn't that a white-power symbol now?"

Richard burst out laughing. "Oh dear, you are on the Internet too much—or too little. No, it isn't a white-power symbol. Well, not really. What happened is that a bunch of right-wing trolls decided to spread that rumor to see if they could get liberals to believe it. Soon it spread like wildfire all over social media and got picked up by the mainstream news. I had white friends on Facebook apologize for using it with me. That was actually the first I'd heard of it. Imagine my confusion. Then some far-right activists who weren't in on the joke started to really use it as a white-power symbol."

Uncle Philip scratched his head. "I don't understand. So it is a white-power symbol, or isn't it?"

"Only if you're a fascist, and considering how

you raised your nephew, I seriously doubt that you are."

"I hadn't heard any of that," Della admitted. "I avoid social media."

"So do I," Lucas said.

Richard spread out his hands. "Ah, another thing you two have in common!"

"Stop," Della and Lucas said together.

Richard chuckled.

"Let's get back to the matter at hand," Montague said. "We know she's been kidnapped, and we know she was alive as of this morning. While that photo tells us little, it does tell us she appears to be unhurt. The kidnappers were also bold enough to take her outside, confident that she wouldn't run."

"She doesn't look drugged in this photo," Della said, zooming in on the image with her phone.

"No, she doesn't," Richard said, leaning over her shoulder and studying it, "and I know a wee bit more about that than you do."

"They probably have guns," Montague said.

"Couldn't this all be a ploy to grab attention?" Della said.

Lucas shook his head. "Just before her lawsuit is due before the court? That doesn't make any sense. She and her legal team fought for years to get the courts to take her case seriously. She wouldn't put that in jeopardy with some stunt that would get her in trouble with the law."

Della considered this for a moment.

"Perhaps she's unstable," she suggested, although her words didn't carry much conviction.

"Her enemies in the palace would like to paint her that way, but did she seem unstable to you?" Montague asked.

"I didn't talk to her for long," Della said.

"Lucas and I have known her for years. She's a bit elitist and drinks more than is good for her, but she's as sane as I am."

The look on Della's face told Lucas that Montague had picked the wrong turn of phrase.

Montague went on, oblivious.

"I did the research you asked of me, Lucas, and found some interesting information. The queen's cousin, George Saxe-Coburg, Duke of Anhalt, is deceased. His commoner lover, Autumn's mother, is also deceased. Autumn is the only child they had together. Now here's where it gets interesting. George Saxe-Coburg was not only in the Saxe-Coburg royal line but was also in another royal line, that of the Principality of Anhalt. For a time, that region of Germany was ruled by a royal line, not just a noble one, and he was descended from that line."

Lucas felt a prickling go down his spine. He glanced at Richard and his aunt, both of whose faces showed they had seen the significance.

"And he was the last of the line?" Lucas asked.

"No, Autumn is," Montague said. "George Saxe-Coburg had only one legitimate child, and he is also deceased. There is no evidence for any other children, legitimate or illegitimate."

"That's all very interesting," Della said, "but could somebody tell me why this is important?"

Lucas turned to her. "As I explained, those with royal blood have magical power. When they are the last of the line, their power intensifies. It's that rarity, that end of an ancient magical line, that makes them a repository of powerful magic."

"So Autumn is a witch?" Della asked.

"I wish you'd stop using that term," Lucas said. "It's imprecise. No, she never showed any magical ability. The Talent is surely there, as Montague discovered when he performed that summoning with her, but he had to guide her. It's more that she can be used as a conduit through which to cast magic."

"What sort of magic?" Della asked. He was surprised she was still following along.

"There are so many different spells that it is impossible to guess what her kidnappers intend, but considering how they grabbed her and how they handled me..." Lucas's hand strayed up to his nose. "You can be sure that their motives are not kind."

Uncle Philip, who, unlike Lucas and Aunt Mary, had no magical ability whatsoever, leaned forward. "Do you think they'll use her as a sacrifice?"

Lucas let out a long sigh. "Quite possibly. Or they might use her for other purposes. Either way, it's serious."

"And either way, she's in serious danger," Montague added. "I had to guide her through the entire ritual. You're right. She has no real magical knowledge of her own. She can be used only as a vessel. And if you overuse such a vessel, it can shatter."

5

THE LAMB STUCK its muzzle through the wire fence and nibbled at the bunch of clover Della held out to it. Uncle Philip had brought in the flock from the pasture for the evening, and they were now all in the enclosure. The sheep were a white, bleating mass that made Della smile. The sight was so different from her usual day-to-day experience, and yet so common, so mundane, it gave her reassurance after the morbid conversation she had had to endure for the last two hours.

She had lapsed into silence and increasing confusion while the others had delved into medieval German royal bloodlines in intricate detail. While it was the sort of academic obscurity that generally intrigued Della, the regular references to magical rituals and entities from the Other Side had turned her off and eventually made her tune out.

Uncle Philip had looked bored, too, and had eventually made his excuses to get back to farm work. She had longed to join him.

Once the meeting broke up, Della had fled out here to get a breath of fresh air. What they had wanted her to do weighed on her. She knew she would get no peace this summer.

"Looks like you made a friend," Uncle Philip said, squishing through the muddy enclosure in his Wellingtons as he brought two large plastic buckets of water to the trough. A few sheep followed him, poking their noses at the buckets to give them a sniff.

Della smiled at him. Funny that she thought of them as "Uncle" Philip and "Aunt" Mary. They were kind and caring in that causal way that close family were, even though Della had only met them less than two months before.

Uncle Philip emptied the buckets as Della offered the lamb another bundle of clover and petted its soft muzzle as it nibbled. The portly old farmer passed through the gate, took care to ensure it was locked behind him, and came over.

"It's all real, you know," he said.

Della didn't reply, instead focusing on the lamb.

Uncle Philip took a deep breath of the warm, fresh evening air and looked out over the broad field enclosed by distant hedges and trees. Evenings are long in the English summer, and even though it was almost eight, there was still plenty of light to see by. Down the hill, the large Tudor house stood silent. From the back they could see no sign of life. That was because, Della knew, they were all up front in the library, poring over old genealogies, trying to trace Autumn's ancient family tree.

"Yes, it's all real," Uncle Philip repeated. "Hard to imagine, isn't it? I've always worked with my hands—farming, pipefitting, woodworking. Lucas learned woodworking from me and became so good at it that I let him take over my workshop. Oh, I can bang together a shed or some bookcases well enough, but he creates works of art. Those replica Georgian pieces go for a pretty penny."

"They're beautiful, all right," Della said, wondering where he was going with all this.

"That, they are," Uncle Philip said with a nod, petting the lamb. "That lad has one foot in this world, and I'm glad of it. But his other foot is firmly set in the unseen world. Mary has got both feet and all the rest of her in that world." He chuckled.

"How did the two of you meet?" Della asked.

They seemed so mismatched and yet so obviously happy together.

"At a party. A friend of mine had invited me to a pagan do out in the woods. I thought he was bonkers, but he was a nice chap and said there would be plenty of free mead and friendly girls. He said that pagan parties were the best, and I daresay he's right. So I went. It was deep in some woods in Essex. Lovely place with a glen and a little lake where people swam. There must have been three hundred people there. Some were friends there just for the party like I was, while others were really serious. They were performing all sorts of rituals and prayer dances. What a load of tosh."

Della laughed. "Don't let your wife hear you say that."

"Oh, she agrees. Most modern pagans just want to smoke dope and make love in the woods. Nothing wrong with that, mind you, but after a couple of days of that, they go back to their semidetached homes and their office jobs and don't give it another thought. It's all just a bit of a laugh, something to make them feel all spiritual and one with the earth while they live like good little urban consumers. Mary wasn't like that, though. Right away I could tell that she was different.

"I spotted her the first day. While my friend and a bunch of the other pagans he knew were dancing around a fire, getting lashed on some excellent home-made mead, I saw her walking through the woods alone, studying each tree as if they were statues in some museum. Ah, she was so pretty! Had on a white dress that came all the way down to her ankles and a little braid of flowers circling her forehead. So I summoned up my courage and went over to say hello."

"Love at first sight?"

Uncle Philip belted out a laugh.

"Not quite. She said, 'Please don't bother me right now. I'm talking with the dryads.'"

Della smiled. "Of all the brushoff lines I've ever heard, that's got to be the most unusual. What did you do?"

"I said, 'Come on over when you're done and tell me what they said.'"

"Was she mad that you made fun of her?"

"Ah, but I didn't," he said, pulling up a handful of grass and feeding it to a curious sheep that had come to the wire fence. "I said this in all seriousness. You see, I had looked in her eyes and saw she wasn't stoned, which is more than I could say for most of the folks there. I also saw that she was in earnest. That got me interested. I wanted to see if she was a nutter or just delusional."

Della nudged him. "Uncle Philip, what a horrible thing to say!"

If he noticed the term "uncle," he didn't let on. "Well, she did say she was chatting with woodland spirits. But it was the way she said it that caught my attention. She wasn't putting on a show like so many of those pagans. I figured either she was crazy or that there might be something more to all this. Turned out there was. A few hours later I was sitting by the fire, and she sat down right next to me. You know what she said? She said, 'The dryads told me you're a good man.' Well, who am I to argue with the dryads?"

Della paused for a moment, looking out over the darkening pasture. Despite Uncle Philip's easygoing, welcoming presence, she felt tense.

"You said this was all real," she whispered.

The farmer nodded. "It took a long time for me to accept it. There's more tosh in this community than real knowledge. Far more. But it is real, Della. I've seen the effect it has on people. I've seen things happen that should never happen if science knew all the facts."

MONTAGUE LEFT THAT NIGHT. The next morning, Lucas, Della, and Richard took the bus back down to London. They spent the hour-long trip sitting in the back row of the bus, out of sight of the other passengers, making plans.

"Remember the ley lines I told you about?" Lucas asked.

"How could I forget? I nearly got killed on one of those damn things."

"So you admit they're real?" Lucas asked with a smile.

"I admit that you think they're real, and the kidnappers probably do too."

"Good enough. Being a royal city, London is crisscrossed with powerful ley lines attuned to royal magic. It would make sense that they would try to use Autumn for a ritual at one of the nodes of some of these ley lines."

"I suppose that makes sense," Della said. "In a completely nonsensical way. How many of these nodes are there?"

"Thirty-three."

"Thirty-three? How the hell are we going to search all of them?"

"That's where you come in. We want you to pick one."

"We have a map of them," Richard said.

"Of course you do."

Richard unfolded a detailed, large-format map of London crisscrossed with straight lines drawn with a pen.

"I'm not even going to ask how you came up with this," Della said.

"Years of investigation by the London Psycho-geographical Society."

Emphasis on the "psycho," Della thought.

"Close your eyes," Lucas said, "and try to empty your mind of all thoughts."

"I don't see how this is going to help Autumn."

"Trust us," Lucas said.

She looked at Lucas, who had saved her life, and Richard, who had helped her through a bad breakup. These two would be perfect friends if they weren't such total loons. Trust them? Yes. Rely on them, only if they were being sensible. Believe in what they said? Not this lifetime.

But they knew more about where the kidnappers were coming from than she ever could.

What was the old saying? "It takes a thief to catch a thief."

She shook her head and closed her eyes.

"Take gentle, deep breaths," Richard said.

"Am I supposed to be meditating here?"

"Something like that."

Della felt tempted to let out a loud *ooommm!* like some yogi. But she was too shy for that. The whole bus would stare. She hoped they weren't staring already. She giggled at the thought.

"Please try to take this seriously," Lucas said. "Autumn is in danger."

I'm the only one who actually is taking this seriously.

She heard a crinkle of paper.

"I've spread out the map in front of you," Richard said. "Now raise your hand, palm down, and pass it back and forth slowly over the map."

"Just relax," Lucas repeated over and over. "Just relax and let your mind be free of thoughts."

She did as she was asked, feeling the smooth surface of the paper under her hand.

And something strange happened.

Maybe it was the stress of the kidnapping. Maybe it was the calm, soothing way that Lucas repeated the instructions. But she felt a strange tingling in her hand, like she was passing it over a grille that gently blew hot air in little jets against her palm.

The tingling spread from her palm along her arm and up to her head, feeling as if a thousand tiny fingers were giving her a scalp message. Instead of being frightened by this or even curious, her calm, detached mind took in this new sensation with complete acceptance.

Again and again she passed her hand over the map, which no longer felt like paper but a topography of warmer and cooler spots. Gradually her hand moved of its own volition to one spot that felt warmer than the rest—almost hot—one spot that felt distinct from all the others.

She forced her hand to pass over the map again, seeking out similar spots, but her hand was inexorably drawn back to that one spot.

Della pulled her hand back and put a finger on that spot, feeling a pulse of warmth travel up her finger.

"Here."

Sudden intakes of breath from Lucas and Richard made her open her eyes.

Her finger rested on a green spot marked Highgate Cemetery.

6

OF ALL THE *places she could have picked.*

Lucas looked nervously around him. The gravestones felt like they were closing in.

Lucas really, really didn't want to be here.

On the surface, Highgate Cemetery was a peaceful, if rather bizarre, sanctuary of quiet in the middle of the big city. Located in a wealthy neighborhood in north London, it had been built in the nineteenth century to deal with the chronic overflow of bodies from London's older cemeteries. It had gotten to the point that bodies were buried two to a coffin and that families paid for plots to be unearthed and the older bones thrown in the Thames to make room for those of their loved ones.

Highgate was reserved for the wealthy, because

even the wealthy couldn't avoid such desecration in those days. This was meant to be a safe place to house the dead, and their tombs reflected the permanence of their social standing in death. Gravel paths shaded by overhanging trees passed between rows of stone sarcophagi. Some were plain, while others were ornately carved with scrollwork and images of long-dead families. More grandiose monuments sported statues of angels. One sad little tomb, barely a meter long, had a sleeping child sculpted in stone lying on top of it. Larger mausoleums with rusty iron gates held entire families from the Victorian age. The greenery grew thick, sometimes almost obscuring the older tombs, and muffled the sounds of traffic from the surrounding city. Passing through Highgate Cemetery made one feel like one had stepped into another world. The entire place exuded a surreal yet peaceful charm.

But that was only on the surface. Deep within, Lucas could feel a troubling disruption in the ley lines that intersected to form a nexus here. Ley lines were powerful lines of earth energy that spanned the globe. When two or more crossed, they created a powerful node that humans instinctively felt at a subconscious level. Most nodes had sacred sites atop them. Highgate Cemetery was the meeting point for three ley lines and was thus extremely potent.

The fact that a burial ground was built here and not a church or stone circle did not bode well.

Dark magic could be done here. Death magic.

Lucas glanced over at Richard. His friend did not look happy.

"Got it in one," Richard said.

Lucas nodded. This was the place, all right.

They were walking along one of the little lanes between the tombs, Della trailing a bit behind.

Richard drew closer to him and whispered, "Do we tell her about the vampire?"

"She's more likely to believe the Easter Bunny moves through this place."

Richard nodded then looked around, his face grim.

"Moving, it most certainly is," he muttered.

"Why are we here?" Della called over to them.

They turned to her.

"You tell us," Lucas said. "You picked this spot."

Della looked impatient. "I picked a spot at random on a map."

Lucas leaned against a half-life-sized statue of a weeping angel on a plinth, which stood slumped over, her stone face looking at him sorrowfully. "You picked one of the most powerful nodes of ley lines in all of London. You did not do that at random."

"Yeah, I did."

"I bet you felt something, didn't you? A bit of heat on the hand, perhaps. And it got warmer when you moved your hand closer to this spot on the map."

Della turned away. "I'm susceptible to suggestion. Whitaker proved that."

"And yet I never suggested it. When did I say that you'd feel heat in your hand?"

"Can you just explain why we're here?" Della snapped.

Lucas summoned his patience and explained it in terms that Della would accept.

"Like with Keaton Whitaker and Dr. Patricia Olding, these people believe in ley lines. This is a particularly strong node for three ley lines, and its association with death makes it especially susceptible to black magic."

"Next you're going to tell me a vampire hangs out here."

Lucas and Richard glanced at each other.

"You don't have to believe," Richard said. "The important thing is that they believe. There's a good chance they might come here."

"So where are they?" Della asked.

The only other people they had seen consisted of a guided tour group that had taken another path.

Lucas shrugged. "I don't know. I doubt they'll come in daylight hours. It's best to check it out now, while it's safe."

Well, relatively safe, he thought.

They wandered the winding paths of the cemetery for the better part of an hour. With more than seventeen thousand people buried in the place, the grounds were extensive. Mostly they walked in silence, admiring the somber beauty of the monuments. Lucas could find no focus point for the disturbed feeling he got from the area.

In a few spots, he spotted some traces of ritual activity. Ribbons adorned the branches of a willow tree in the old pagan style. The stubs of burnt-out candles stuck in blobs of wax on some of the graves. And he found the remains of a pentagram that had been written with coal dust. This, however, was faded and half blown away by the wind. He passed his hand over it and felt nothing. Richard focused on it for a time and got no sensations from it either. It had most likely been left by some amateur occultists. Those they were hunting wouldn't be so ineffective.

"So where are they?" Della asked again, clearly impatient.

"I didn't think we'd stand much of a chance at finding them during the day," Lucas admitted. "They'll most likely come at night."

"Isn't this place closed at night?"

"Well, yes."

Della cocked her head and frowned. "You're not suggesting what I think you're suggesting, are you?"

SEVERAL HOURS LATER, after meeting up with Montague, who had been poring over obscure tomes in the British Library, and having a dinner during which Della looked increasingly troubled, they went back to Highgate Cemetery.

It was now ten in the evening, and the last glimmerings of twilight were fading away to the west. The street outside of the cemetery was quiet, with only the occasional resident or black taxi cab passing by. The four of them strolled up the lane, which was bounded on one side by the high iron fence enclosing the cemetery and on the other by few shops, all dark and shut at this hour. The fence was topped with spikes. Inside, all was swathed in darkness. The greenery cooled the air of the summer evening.

Lucas shivered a little and wished he had brought along a pullover.

"How are we going to get in?" Della asked. It had taken several hours of arguing to get her to agree to this. It had taken an equal amount of time for Lucas to convince himself.

Montague smiled. "There's a padlock on the gate. I'll pick it quickly enough."

"This isn't a game of Dungeons and Dragons. You can't just pick a lock," Della said.

"Careful," the book dealer said. "You just outed yourself as a nerd. And no, I'm not some fantasy character. I'm a trained locksmith. That was my day job until I could find my feet in the rare book trade."

In the dim light of the streetlamps, Lucas couldn't tell if Della had blushed, but he could guess.

"So are you an elf or a hobbit?" Richard asked.

"Shut up."

Richard and Montague snickered. Lucas suppressed a smile.

"Maybe she'll use her magic sword to save us all," Montague said.

"It's a game," Della grumbled. "At least I don't think this stuff is real."

"You'll come around," Richard said in a singsong voice.

They got to the gate. A CCTV camera was fixed to a high pole right next to it. Automatically everyone hunched over and kept their faces averted.

"We can't break in," Della said. "We'll be filmed."

"Oh, those aren't monitored," Montague replied. "As long as we leave things the way we found them, they won't have any reason to look back at the footage."

"They are so monitored. I saw it on an ITV documentary," Della said.

"The same channel that brought us *Celebrity Love Island*? Please. That's a lie meant to make us feel safer. The only CCTV cameras that are continuously monitored are the ones in the financial district and outside the major nightclubs. London has thousands of CCTV cameras. There simply isn't the manpower to watch all of them."

Della looked half-convinced but grumbled, "I have a bad feeling about this."

So did Lucas but not because of the camera. The strange sense of movement in the ley lines felt stronger now. This was a night place, and not all the spirits laid to rest here actually rested.

Montague pulled a leather pouch from inside his

tweed jacket and opened it. Inside were various lockpicks.

"Whoa, you're serious about this," Della said.

"I'm serious about everything I say," Montague replied as he got to work.

Twice he had to stop as cars approached. When this happened, they all walked away as if they were simply passing along the road. When the cars went out of sight, they hurried back to the gate, and Montague fiddled with the lock again.

After a few minutes, he got it. He popped off the lock, unwrapped the chain with a rattle, and creaked open the gate.

Just then, the headlights of a car appeared and quickly grew brighter as it came up the lane.

"Get in!" Montague urged them.

They rushed into the cemetery. As soon as Lucas entered, he felt like he had pushed through an invisible wall of cold, like he had just opened the door to a meat locker. But it was more than that. It was a physical thing. The others must have felt it too.

Ignoring the clammy sense of dread that chilled him to the core, he moved with the others farther into the cemetery to get out of sight of the street. Lucas ducked behind a tree as the light from the car brightened. Montague stayed behind to throw the chain

back around the gate to make it look like it was undis-
turbed and then bolted for the shadows just before
the car went past.

After it dimmed into the distance, Lucas saw him
creep out of the shadows and put the lock back
through the chain.

"What's he doing that for?" Della asked. She had
chosen the same tree to hide behind.

"I guess he wants to make it look more natural,"
Lucas said.

"What is he? A housebreaker or something?"

"No, but I am a heartbreaker," Montague said,
strolling up.

"I find that rather unlikely," Richard said,
appearing out of the shadow of a tomb.

"You're quite safe from me, Richard," Montague
grumbled.

"Trust me. I wasn't offering," Richard replied.

"Quiet," Lucas said.

"Do you hear something?" Della asked, looking
around fearfully.

For a moment, everyone remained quiet. No, he
didn't hear anything. He sure felt something, though.
The initial sense of cold dread he had felt when they
passed through the gate remained. He couldn't

locate any center. Instead it was more of a general aura.

Magic had been cast here and not the good kind.

"Why's it so cold?" Della whispered.

Lucas didn't bother answering. She would figure it out on her own soon enough.

Without a word, Lucas led them deeper into the cemetery. The crunching of their feet sounded agonizingly loud in the still night. Lucas felt tempted to walk on the grass, but tripping over a tombstone in the dark was not a risk he relished.

"What are we looking for?" Della asked.

"I'm not sure. I don't think they're here yet."

"Won't they notice Montague picked the lock?"

"No," the book dealer said. "I locked it behind us."

Della stopped and spun to face him. "Are you crazy? You just locked us in a cemetery in the middle of the night?"

"If I had left it open, all sorts of bad people might have come in."

"Like the police," Richard added.

"How will this supposed cult of royal kidnappers get in?" Della asked.

"I'm sure they have a way," Lucas said.

Della sighed and muttered something under her breath as they kept going.

The sky was clear, the faint glow of the city diffusing the stars. The blinking lights of a low-flying airplane passed overhead, no doubt headed for Heathrow or Gatwick. The reminder that they were in the middle of a modern city carried little weight. Inside the bounds of this cemetery, they were very much in their own world.

"This place is beautiful in a creepy sort of way," Della murmured.

She had moved a bit ahead, Lucas and the others falling in behind but keeping a respectful distance. Lucas had the feeling her latent talent might be leading them somewhere.

Della stopped at a tombstone. It had been sculpted in the shape of a pyramid with a sphinx in front.

"It suits you," Richard said and chuckled. Lucas elbowed him.

"These hieroglyphs are fake."

"Well, la-di-da."

"Quiet, Richard," Lucas whispered.

"I'm keeping her at ease to let her subconscious find whatever it is she's looking for," he whispered back.

Della moved on, following the path's gentle curve between the weird and varied tombstones. There was no moon, and the streetlight did not penetrate this far in, but the ambient light of the vast unseen city around them illuminated their way.

Lucas felt a growing sense of dread. It was not from any sensation that there had been a further disturbance in the ley lines but more of something remembered, something he had heard a long time ago.

It was a lecture he had attended at one of the many occult circles in London, about events that had happened here almost fifty years ago.

Richard swore under his breath.

"What?" Lucas asked.

"I think she's leading us to the crypt."

And suddenly Lucas remembered. It had been a meeting of the London Occult Circle, a grim and suspicious crowd of people who wore far too much black and who had made him so uneasy that he swore never to return. The talk, in the back room of a pub with the door locked, had ranged from curses to animal sacrifice. He loathed people who twisted the magical arts to such purposes.

The evening's talk, however, had been instructive.

It had been about the so-called Highgate Vampire.

The speaker, an elderly man who had been one of the psychic investigators during the original case, explained that it had started with newspaper reports in 1969 of ghost sightings in the cemetery. Back then it wasn't as well guarded, and it was used as a hangout for young people to smoke grass or make out, although the idea of making out in a cemetery left Lucas feeling rather queasy. A tall man wearing dark clothes and a top hat was seen on numerous occasions, as were people reporting groans and muffled screams or the sound of distant bells. People walking along adjoining Swain's Lane were sometimes startled by a pale face grinning at them through the bars.

Some nutter had written to the papers, saying it was the king of the vampires, and the tabloid press, ever desperate for a juicy story, had a field day. Self-styled vampire hunters swore they would kill the creature, and the police had to be called in to stop young men armed with wooden stakes from desecrating the graves.

The case might have been laughed off as an episode of mass hysteria, except one night, the body of a woman was found in the cemetery. It had been burnt to a crisp, and the head was missing. No one was ever arrested for the crime. Someone had been casting some very dark magic in Highgate Cemetery.

The speaker, whose name escaped him, had insisted that it had been a case of real-life vampirism. Lucas had dismissed the idea of the entity actually being a human who had risen from the dead to suck to blood of the living. Such things did not happen. He thought that it might instead be a spirit that someone had summoned and lacked the Talent to dismiss. It happened sometimes, if the stars were right and the spirit strong enough. It explained many hauntings and possessions, at least those that hadn't been made up by schizophrenics or publicity seekers.

The pull of the spirit world was strong, though, and the spirit was not in its natural element in our world. So in time it would fade back into its own dimension. And the Highgate "Vampire" had been active more than forty years ago. Lucas had assumed that if it had existed at all, it would be long gone.

Now he wasn't so sure.

7

DELLA WALKED SLOWLY along the path, the only sound she heard being the steady crunch of gravel under her feet. The distant buzz of the city had faded away. She was dimly aware that the others weren't by her anymore, but she did not turn her head to see if they were following.

What lay ahead was far more interesting.

This was a beautiful place. Alluring. Worries about Autumn and the kidnappers and the police passed from her thoughts as her mind emptied. There was only this strange compulsion to move forward.

The angels on the gravestones seemed to watch her as she came to a fork in the path and chose the left-hand turning, feeling certain that this was the correct way.

The correct way to what? She never gave it a thought.

Trees and shrubbery closed in on either side. The gravel ended, and she walked along a dirt path, stepping over tangled roots. Once, she stumbled, having to grab at the head of a stone child lying in eternal rest atop its undersized sarcophagus. For a second, she woke up, as if having been hit by an electrical charge, and felt a spike of fear and disorientation. Then she righted herself, took a deep breath, and continued down the path.

As it curved and narrowed between the enclosing greenery, there came into view an ornate marble mausoleum looking as pale as bone in the city's ambient light. The doorway was a rectangle of black. A mausoleum with an open door? The strangeness of it briefly rose and faded from her mind.

She approached, a subtle sense of dread beginning to rise in her benumbed body. Her footsteps faltered, and for a moment, the fear felt like it would overcome her until she gazed into that rectangle of pitch black, an open doorway that seemed to grow bigger of its own volition to encompass her entire vision, and the feeling faded away. She needed to enter.

Before she knew it, she had. Vaguely she felt cold metal in her hand and heard the echoing booms of a heavy door shutting, and all was dark.

No. A distant light shone ahead and below her. No longer feeling her body, Della moved toward this light. She didn't know whether she was still walking or being carried. She did not even think to ask these things.

The light grew, sparkling. Della made out a white shape that glowed faintly. The reflection of that glow rippled on a pool of dark water.

It was a girl, a few years younger than she was, with long blond hair tied in a plait down her back. She was kneeling by the water. As Della approached, she looked up and smiled.

Della stood before her, unable to speak because she could not think of any words. She wasn't sure words worked in a place such as this.

The girl dipped her hand in the water and raised it. The glow emanating from her pale skin shone through the water, a little pool of radiance, given as an offering.

Drink.

It was not said, and it was not a command. It was

an invitation, communicated in some way other than speech.

Della leaned forward. Her mouth slowly opened.

The girl's eyes widened. She shrank back, looking at something beyond Della's shoulder. The girl raised her hands to protect herself, and the offering of water splashed at her feet.

The dread returned, prickling up Della's back like a thousand icy cockroaches. She felt herself tense and hunch over. Something was behind her, something close. The vision of the girl receded, dwindling into the distance as if Della were looking at her from the rearview mirror of a moving car.

And then the girl and her light were gone, and all that was left for Della was darkness and dread.

She found she could move again, that her body was her own once more. But she did not want to move. The thing behind her demanded attention, and she did not dare look at it.

Turn around.

This time it was not an invitation but a command and far more powerful than the girl with the water.

Della tried with every fiber of her being not to look at what she was commanded to see. She tensed every muscle to keep from turning.

But turn she did.

And froze.

Right in front of her loomed a tall figure in a long dark coat and top hat. His face shone like the girl's, but instead of a pure-white glow, it shone with a sickly light that reminded Della of a dusty old light bulb encrusted with dead flies. His face was long and pale, the features sharp. He grinned, showing rotten, irregular teeth.

The most arresting feature was the eyes. They were penetrating and of the palest blue. They gazed at her hungrily as he reached out a hand.

And then all went black.

8

LUCAS SAW Della turn and look out of the doorway of the mausoleum. She was looking right at them, but her gaze was far away. Lucas was sure she did not see him running for the door when she slammed it shut and slid the bolt.

Lucas ran up to the door and pounded on it. "Della, open up!"

"It's no good, Lucas," Richard said, coming up beside him. "Montague, can you open that bolt?"

"In a tightly flush steel door? No. It isn't a door chain."

"Della!" Lucas pounded again then turned to Montague. "Any other way in?"

"Possibly. This way." Montague turned and ran back down the path.

He led them out of the gate, quickly picking the lock and fixing the chain behind them, before circling to the other side of the park, where a side lane angled steeply down to an intersection. Montague kept up a fast pace, his long legs eating up the distance, and Lucas found he was sweating from more than worry by the time they got to the bottom of the hill.

"Look," Montague said, extending a bony arm along the intersecting street. It ran at the base of the slope on which Highgate sat, all the way past the end of the cemetery.

"Who lives downhill from a cemetery?" Richard asked.

"No one interesting, sadly. I checked. The real estate is wasted on them."

Montague led them along the street, glancing up the slope and then ahead before glancing a moment later up the slope again.

"Where are we going?" Lucas asked, brimming with impatience.

"Just about... here." Montague stopped, pointing at an old pub called The Red Lion. It was as dark and shut as the homes along the street. "This is directly downhill from the mausoleum."

"How can you know?"

"I estimated. Oh, I might be off a few meters either way, but that would put us in that private home there or the little car park there. Since even you know that it isn't the car park—as you can see, there are no manhole covers—and I don't fancy breaking into a private home, we should check the cellar of that pub."

"For?" Lucas asked.

Montague rolled his eyes. "You really must come down for a season. You would learn so many things." He walked over to the front door of the pub, studied the security-system sticker on the frame, pulled out his lockpicks, and got to work. "This area had an early Victorian drainage system put in. One of the first. The firm didn't get off the ground financially and thus didn't leave many of these systems. They were put on various spots of high ground as an aid to sewage and rainwater runoff. Ah! Here we go."

Montague popped the lock and was about to push it open when Richard stopped him.

"There's an alarm system. You saw it."

"I probably know the code."

"Probably?"

"Probably. If I'm wrong, we run."

Lucas and Richard both nodded, neither looking happy.

Montague eased open the door and entered a small foyer, stepping to the glowing security panel on the wall. He punched a number into a keypad set below a red light.

It let out a little negative beep. Lucas and Richard moved to run, but Montague extended a hand.

"Wait."

He punched another set of numbers. Another beep.

"Look, we need to find another—"

"Do be quiet. I'm trying to concentrate," Montague murmured and punched in another number.

The red light turned to green. Montague urged them inside. They shut the door quietly behind them as Montague opened a glass door just beyond the security panel to enter the pub proper.

Lucas squinted, trying to see. The shades were all drawn, and besides a few little lights on equipment behind the bar, there was no illumination. He pulled out his phone and turned it on.

"There," Richard said, pointing to a door behind the bar. "That must lead to the cellar."

"Very good," Montague said, grinning. "Trust you to know your way around a pub."

Lucas was in too much of a hurry to slap him upside the head. He crept as quickly as he could around the bar and opened the door. Steep stairs led down a brick shaft. The smell of damp rose to him like a slap in the face by a clammy towel. He started to descend. Richard followed. Lucas heard Montague clear his throat behind him. He turned around.

Montague still stood at the top of the stairs. He gave them a bashful look and whispered, "I'll... I'll guard the door."

Lucas hesitated a second then whispered back, "Oh, all right. Call to us if the landlord comes down. His will be the flat upstairs."

"I do go to pubs sometimes, you know," Montague said as Lucas and Richard continued down the stairs.

The cellar was a cramped little room about ten feet by ten under a low brick vault. Behind a pile of metal beer kegs was a wall covered with plywood.

"There we go," Lucas said, putting his phone in his pocket, and grabbed a keg. "Help me with these."

He found it was full.

"It must weigh sixty pounds at least. We'll never get all these out quietly," Lucas said.

Richard had turned on his own phone and bent

down. It was only then that Lucas noticed the kegs were stacked on low steel trolleys. Richard flipped the safety off each of the corner wheels, put his phone on top of the nearest keg, and pulled the whole stack away.

"You need to think with your head more often than other things, Lucas," Richard said.

"Come on. Help me with this!"

Lucas squeezed past the stack of kegs before Richard had entirely pulled it away and went to the plywood along the wall. The damp had warped the edges and pulled the nails halfway out of the frame. It only took a hard tug to pull it free.

A hard and loud tug. The nails squeaked in the damp wood, and the bottom part banged against Lucas's foot as it came free.

He saw Richard cringe and heard a sharp "Psst!" from the top of the stairs.

A warning or just telling them to be quiet? Lucas wasn't about to call up and ask. That really would wake up the landlord.

Richard helped him move the plywood aside and saw it had been nailed to a firmer frame of aged wooden beams. Beyond ran a dank tunnel barely big enough to walk through.

It was at this moment that Richard's phone

decided to turn off. Lucas flinched, digging into his pocket for his phone with one hand and holding the other out in case something came at them.

"Christ!" Richard whispered. Lucas heard fumbling, then the light came back on.

Lucas pulled out his own phone, and they shined them down the passage. It ran for a few steps before it came to another passage angling downward. The faint trickle of running water came to their ears.

It took just a moment to hunch through the low passageway to its end, where they found themselves standing on a slick ledge of worn brick. The tunnel they had come to was larger, a tube of arched brick running from up the slope, down under the pub's cellar, and through an arch to disappear in the darkness. A thin sheen of water flowing down the tunnel floor hinted at an underground river somewhere farther down. On either side of the sloping tunnel ran a narrow walkway. Two steps cut into the wall allowed Lucas to get onto one of them. He shined his light down the slope, probing the darkness beyond the arch beneath the pub cellar. Water glimmered in his far vision. He turned and shined the light up. The tunnel continued until it was almost out of sight. Beyond, he spotted vague shapes. Bulky. Unmoving.

"I think I heard Montague call to us again," Richard whispered. He was still on the ledge, looking back down the passage to the pub cellar.

"If we need to run, it's too late to run any way but this way," Lucas said. Now that he had found a possible way to find Della, he didn't think of his own safety.

The path was narrow and slick with damp, but the builders had left the surface roughly hewn to give the feet grip. He steadied himself with his free hand, the bricks slimy to the touch. Richard came right behind him. As they walked up, the shapes in the wavering light of their phones resolved into a ledge, beyond which opened a cellar similar in size and shape to the one in the pub, although with very different contents.

Two large lead sarcophagi stood side by side. Della stood with her hand resting on one, her face a blank.

Cold washed through Lucas's body and not just from fear. Magic had been cast here. He could feel it. Richard's clenched jaw and wide eyes told Lucas that he felt it too.

Carefully he stepped up to Della and studied her. His face was barely a hand's breadth from hers, and yet her eyes remained fixed and unseeing.

"Is this a spell?" Lucas asked.

"She's under some sort of psychic control," Richard said.

He shined the light from his phone right in her face. Della made no reaction. Her pupils didn't even contract.

Lucas struggled to remain calm and glanced down at the sarcophagus on which her hand rested.

Ebenezer King

Never Born. Passed to another plane December 31, 1839

He looked over at the other lead-lined sarcophagus on the opposite side of the small chamber.

Cordelia King, wife of Ebenezer

Born June 21, 1821. Died December 31, 1839

"Oh no," Richard whispered, staring at the sarcophagi.

"What?"

"We've got to get out of here. Now. Wake her up."

Lucas took Della by the shoulders and shook her gently, calling her name. No response.

"Come on, Della, wake up," he said, shaking her a bit harder. She felt stiff, her face a blank.

A cold wind blew through the crypt, cutting

through Lucas like he wasn't there. For a second, he wondered where the draft was coming from.

Until he realized it wasn't wind at all. It was a spirit sucking the heat out of the surrounding air in order to manifest itself.

No time to be gentlemanly. Lucas slapped Della across the face. This elicited a little grunt. Della's eyes went from staring into the far distance to being unfocused, trying to fix on something. The corner of her mouth twitched.

"We got to go now!" Richard said.

He grabbed Della by one arm as Lucas grabbed her by the other, and they hauled her away from the sarcophagus and toward the steps leading up to the entrance of the crypt. Her body tried to resist, showing surprising strength, and they had to all but carry her.

The chill grew worse, clutching at Lucas's heart and turning his legs to water. He looked back over his shoulder.

In the far corner of the crypt, the figure of a tall man in a dark coat and top hat resolved itself out of the shadows.

9

DELLA WOKE UP RUNNING. She had the vague sensation of stumbling up a flight of steps and yet somehow not falling until she realized she had two strong arms under her own. Someone was screaming right next to her. She began to find her feet on a dirt path that a moment later she recognized as being one she had walked a while before in the cemetery. Blinking, she was finally able to look clearly around her and saw it was Lucas and Richard holding her. By the time they got to the gravel portion, she could just manage to support herself on wobbly legs. Lucas still held one arm. She let him, expecting to fall at any moment.

A cold wind blowing from behind made her tremble. She began to turn her head to look, but

Lucas put a hand on her cheek and pushed her to face forward.

"Don't look at it. That's what it wants!"

"That's what *what* wants?" she asked, her words coming out mumbled and unclear.

She thought she knew and shuddered, nearly stumbling.

Richard's voice came from behind them. "Begone! Begone! Three times I tell you, begone!"

This was followed by a string of nonsense words. It sounded a bit like Latin but mixed in with some other language Della did not know.

They ran. The cold subsided. Richard appeared beside them, stumbling even more than she was.

"I put a lot of power into that," he said, "but it won't hold it long."

They came to the gate as Della was finally coming to her full senses. Montague stood on the other side, uncoiling the chain.

"What are you doing out there?" she asked. Through the fog in her brain, she realized how ridiculous her words sounded.

"Come on" was all he said as he creaked the gate open.

Through the trees and shadows of the cemetery, they suddenly saw blue and white lights flashing.

"They're at the pub," Lucas said. "Montague, come on."

He was still fumbling to put the lock through the chain.

Della looked around blearily. Pub? What did that have to do with anything? What was going on?

"One minute," he said. He snapped the lock shut, pulled out a handkerchief, and rubbed down the lock and chain.

A chill ran through her.

"It's coming!" Richard said. "Hurry up!"

Montague finished, looked into the cemetery, and squawked.

"Bloody hell! What did you people do?"

They hurried up a side street, taking them in the opposite direction from where the police lights flashed.

As they put some distance between them and the cemetery, the chill began to fade. Della felt an insatiable curiosity to look behind her. She didn't even think about it. It was as if an unseen hand turned her head.

From between the bars of the wrought-iron fence, a pale face gazed at her hungrily.

Della screamed. She should have bolted but instead found herself rooted in place. Lucas grabbed her arm and yanked her nearly off her feet, forcing her to look away and keep running.

She tried to tell them what she had seen. Her throat clamped, and the words would not come out.

"What if another patrol car comes round?" she heard Richard ask, sounding as if he was far away. The world had faded around her, and she had to lean on Lucas to keep from falling.

"This gets us to a street that's reasonably busy even at this hour," Montague said. "We'll just merge with the crowd. The landlord only saw me, so once there, I'll break up with you and meet up with you later."

Della turned to Lucas, finally getting her mouth to form words.

"I'm exhausted. Let's get back home. The bus runs twenty-four hours," she said. She had to get away from this place. The farther the better. She wanted to be home.

Montague shook his head. "We have much work to do tomorrow. It would be better if you stayed in London and if we all stayed together. Safety in numbers. You can stay at my house. Della can have the spare room, and the study has a foldaway bed. Lucas and Richard, you'll have to draw lots to see who gets the living-room sofa."

Della rubbed her temples, still trying to sort out what had happened. She had gone into the mausoleum. Someone had been there. And then Richard and Lucas had been hauling her up a flight of steps. And that face between the bars ...

"Thank you for the offer, but really, I think we should be getting back to Oxford," she said.

Home. She needed her cozy little flat and familiar bed and about three days of books and solitude.

"Don't worry," Montague said. "I won't make an attempt on your virtue. I'm sure if I did, Lucas would come swinging in like Tarzan. I only hope Richard doesn't make an attempt on mine."

"You're quite safe with me," Richard said in a tone that expressed his utter repulsion to the idea.

"You won't steal the silverware either, will you, old boy?"

"I've seen your silverware. Old-fashioned hand-me-downs with little resale value."

Montague clapped. "Then it's been decided. I'll make you all a nice fry-up in the morning, and we can get back to work refreshed."

Della couldn't understand why they were engaging in banter after what had just happened, and she didn't want to spend the night at Montague's house, but she was too tired to argue. Just before they got to the busier street, Montague told them to meet him at Euston station in half an hour and hurried off in another direction. They caught a night bus heading east to the station. Being inside a lit bus with other people and hearing normal conversation helped bring Della back to her senses. Highgate Cemetery felt like some sort of bad dream. The confusing memories of it began to fade. She found herself looking at all the normal people in the bus doing normal things—that sleepy-eyed woman obviously coming home from a late shift, the slightly drunk businessmen talking too loudly, the teenage couple whispering and giggling to each other. Here was real life, normal life, the kind of life she had never entirely fit in with. The kind of life she hoped she would finally join by going to a new university in a new country.

Instead she found herself blacking out after breaking into a cemetery in the middle of the night.

They met Montague at the entrance to the train station, the courtyard out front still buzzing with late-night travelers, small groups of drunks, and the homeless bedding down for the night.

"It's not far," the bookseller said, "and it's a sight

better than sleeping on a length of cardboard out here. It's supposed to rain later."

Montague's house was as odd as its owner. An old Georgian-era relic in Bloomsbury, not far from where Lucas and Della had gone to the book fair, it stood on Bedford Square, just west of the British Museum. Della had been to the square before, attracted by a mention by one of the other graduate students that it was one of the few eighteenth-century London squares that remained intact.

At this hour, it was abandoned. The ornate wrought-iron streetlamps, converted from gas to electricity a hundred years ago, shone on brick facades turned a dark brown by generations of smog. Tidy rows of tall windows looked out over a lush garden of bushes, trees, and benches in the square's center, fenced off by a tall ironwork fence not unlike the one that protected Highgate Cemetery. The gate had a sign declaring, Access Restricted to Local Residents Only. Such was the case for many of the city's green areas. Only those who could afford to live in the neighborhood could enjoy them.

Bedford Square was one of the highest-rent districts in London, and Della had never expected to meet anyone who lived here. Certainly not a shabbily dressed and poorly socialized occult bookseller like Montague.

Their host came to one of the narrower houses and ascended a few stone steps up to a green door festooned with an ornate brass door knocker shaped like a coiled dragon. He opened the door and, with a furtive glance around the square, ushered everyone inside.

Despite her exhaustion, Della could not help but admire the interior. To the right of a short entrance hallway that led to a steep flight of steps stood the sitting room, furnished with overstuffed antique armchairs and a round oak table littered with books. The walls were all lined with floor-to-ceiling book-shelves. It looked like a smaller version of Aunt Mary's library.

Beyond that was a dining room that could have used a bit of dusting and a lounge that was almost entirely taken up by books stacked on the floor, rising at times to block out the bookshelves along the wall. The only open space was a path from the doorway to a large, sagging leather sofa with several little splits in the arms. Two especially large book piles were on either side of an adjoining armchair, looking like twin columns framing the sitter. A smaller and tidier back room had a desk, more bookshelves, and a sofa that Richard began to pull out into a bed.

"You're upstairs," Montague told Della. "I'll show you around and put on some tea."

Della was relieved when Lucas and Richard came up too.

The upstairs had a small landing leading to two bedrooms, a bathroom, and a spare room. One bedroom Della only saw through the door. A rumpled bed stood in the middle of the room, with a nightstand piled with books. Several old socks lay scattered on the floor. Montague led her to the other bedroom. It smelled musty and was obviously unused except for yet another bookshelf and some cardboard boxes taking up one corner.

Della didn't care. There was a bed.

Beside the bathroom was a third room, the strangest Della had ever seen.

It was entirely filled with locks.

Locks were set on wooden frames like portraits on the walls. A large table taking up most of the room was covered by small blocks of wood with locks set in them.

Montague grinned and wiggled his fingers. "One has to keep in practice."

As he chuckled at his own joke, he showed Della the linen closet and headed downstairs to make tea.

Once she had gathered what she needed, she splashed her face with cold water in the sink. Although fatigue still pulled her down like lead weights, her thoughts were clearer now. Fragments of memory, snatches of sound, and flashes of imagery tried to assemble themselves into some coherent picture in her mind. It still didn't make sense, though. Who had been in that mausoleum, and why had she felt so strange before entering it?

She hesitated at the top of the stairs, listening to the animated conversation of the three strange men in the kitchen. Phrases like "psychic energy" and "blood ritual" filtered up to her.

The bedroom beckoned. Maybe she should just go to sleep and let the guys babble on. But no, that would only delay the inevitable. She might as well go down and hear their crackpot theory now instead of over breakfast tomorrow.

As she entered the kitchen, where the three of them sat around a chipped Formica table, Montague was just pouring tea.

"I took the liberty of making you a special herbal blend of my own making," Montague said to her as she came in. "It will soothe you. I daresay you don't want any caffeine at this hour. Your spirit needs rest."

She slumped into a chair next to Lucas and gratefully took the steaming cup their host handed her. After a couple of sips of the delicate- and earthy-tasting liquid, Lucas turned to her.

"So what do you remember?"

Della shook her head and frowned. "It's all so vague. I remember feeling strange while I was walking through the cemetery. I knew you guys were right behind me, but for some reason, I felt like I was alone. Then I came to the mausoleum, and I sort of blacked out. There was a light and someone crouching by the water and a tall figure."

A sudden shudder shook Della's entire body, making her slosh the tea out of her cup. It burnt her finger, and she dropped the cup, cracking it and splashing the rest of the tea on the table.

"Oh, sorry!" She tried to mop it up with a napkin.

"No matter," Montague said in a soothing voice. "Think nothing of it. The cup is of a mismatched set I got at a charity shop. Better run that finger under some cold water. Here."

He led her to the sink and turned on the tap. While the cool flow of water soothed her finger, she trembled at the dim memories lurking in the recesses of her mind. Montague fetched another cup, filled it with more tea, and set it down at her place.

"Now I really think you should drink this one."

Della nodded and drank in silence for a time. The others said nothing either. After a while, the lack of conversation made her feel awkward. They were obviously waiting for her to speak.

"I can't remember any more. There seemed to have been two people. The one by the water, a girl, wasn't threatening. The other..." Her hand shook a little, and her words trailed off.

"Did he hurt you? Threaten you?" Lucas asked.

"I don't think so. It was more the way he looked. It doesn't make any sense, but he just sort of radiated evil."

The three men glanced at one another as if this were significant.

"Did you guys see them?"

"No," Richard said. "All we saw was you entering the mausoleum and slamming the door behind you. Then you bolted it."

"I did what?"

"You didn't look yourself," Lucas said. "Your eyes were a million miles away."

Della tried to digest this bit of information, and

her mind came up a blank. "I don't remember doing that. Why would I do that?"

"You were under that spirit's control," Montague said. "We all felt its presence. When you locked yourself in, we had to find another way under the cemetery. I've long thought there were underground tunnels there. There was a lot of research around the cemetery in the 1970s, and many of the older investigators here in London remember coming across tunnels. So I went to the most likely entry point, and we were fortunate enough to find you."

"Except first we had to break into a pub and have the police called on us," Lucas said.

Della rolled her eyes. "This is the last time I go buy rare books with you. And before you say anything more about spirits, I'm going upstairs and going to bed."

The others didn't try to stop her. As she left the kitchen, she saw Montague preparing more tea. It looked like they were going to be up for a while.

Back in her room, Della found with relief that there was a chain on the door. She made sure it was securely in place. Then she thought of the room with the locks and how easily Montague had opened the padlock at Highgate Cemetery. The chain wouldn't prove much of a problem. Some kind of thin, hooked instrument could reach around and pull it off.

There was a little desk to one side with a chair. She put the chair against the door and set a dusty glass she found on the desk on the very edge of the chair.

Now all she had to worry about was what might be living in that musty old bed.

She checked the sheets, found them cleaner than she expected but not as clean as she would have liked, and climbed in. For a time, she couldn't sleep. She'd get just to the brink of dreaming, the time when images flashed through one's mind in between more lucid moments, and each time, the images would be from the mausoleum and would snap her awake.

Most were of the tall figure. Some, even more frightening, were of... other things.

But at last she felt herself being pulled to sleep. The images faded, and for the second time in a few hours, she was carried away into darkness.

10

WHEN DELLA CAME DOWN to breakfast at nine the next morning, the other three had already finished and were sitting around the chipped old Formica table, having a second cup of tea.

"Feel better?" Lucas asked.

"Yes. I slept like a log," Della said, still looking drowsy.

"Bacon, eggs, and toast?" Montague asked.

"Thank you. I'm starving," she said, slumping into a chair.

"Are things a little clearer?" Lucas asked.

She nodded. "Still confused about last night. Did I get hypnotized or something?"

"You were possessed," Lucas said.

"Oh, come on!"

"Then how do you explain your actions?"

Della gave a little shrug, suddenly unsure. Then she shuddered and hugged herself.

"That man, the tall one in the long coat and top hat. He hypnotized me somehow. Just like my professor and her lover. You said you found me in a daze. That must have been a hypnotic trance. I'm thinking some of you occultists have learned a special type of hypnotism, something far more powerful than what most people know about. You probably keep the technique a secret. Even psychotherapists don't know about it. That's how you make all your tricks and make people believe in magic."

Montague chuckled as he fussed over the stove. Lucas and Richard exchanged glances.

"Let's go with that theory for the moment," Lucas said. "Say this fellow hypnotized you. Any idea why?"

She shook her head. "It was all so vague. He didn't hurt me, and I don't remember him saying anything. Then there was that girl kneeling by the water. I don't know if she was real or a thought planted in my head or what."

Montague turned and looked at her curiously.

"Why do you think she might not have been real but the man in the long coat was?"

Della shuddered again. "Oh, he was real, all right. He followed us to the edge of the cemetery and watched us through the fence."

Montague served her breakfast, and she ate in silence. They gave her some distance. She obviously needed to recover.

And Lucas needed to think. The events of the previous night still didn't make much sense, but they had obviously stumbled upon the remains of a powerful ritual. The spirit that had been dubbed the Highgate "Vampire" fifty years before had been summoned again. If Richard hadn't cast a banishing spell at it before it had fully manifested, the thing would have surely caught them.

It almost had anyway.

What it wanted with Della remained a mystery. Had it called her there? Was that why she chose that particular nexus of ley lines on the map? And what connection did that have to Autumn's abduction?

Lucas shifted nervously in his seat. Was Autumn even still alive? More than a day had passed, and here they sat drinking tea, getting nothing done. His gut squirmed with impatience.

At least they knew one thing—the identity of the Highgate Vampire. Richard had told him the previous night once they had made it to the safety of this house that he had recognized the name on the sarcophagus. Ebenezer King had been a leading occultist in his day and the one with the worst reputation. There had been rumors of blood rituals and human sacrifices. Several times, the authorities had investigated him, but his wealth and his political connections kept him safe.

And now someone had summoned him.

And Ebenezer King knew who they were.

As the others showered and got ready for the day, Montague went to the corner shop for a few groceries. When he came back, he had a newspaper sticking out of his shopping bag and a frown on his face.

"Look at this," he said.

He pulled out a copy of the *Daily Mirror* and opened it to page five.

"Return of the Vampire?" a headline blared. Underneath the bold print was the subheading "Highgate Cemetery Pub Break-In, Secret Tunnel Found to Mausoleum."

Richard groaned.

"At least we're not on the cover," Lucas said.

"But they do have pictures." Montague held the

newspaper up. The short article was illustrated with three grainy black-and-white pictures, obviously stills from the street's CCTV cameras. One showed all of them together at the cemetery gate as Montague picked the lock. Another showed him doing the same at the door to the Red Lion pub. A third, from an interior camera, showed them moving through the pub's main room.

All were typically unclear. The one at the cemetery gate was taken from an elevated position and well down the street. It was hard even to tell that there were three men and a woman, although Montague's notable height stood out. The one in front of the pub was clearer. Luckily all three of them had kept their heads lowered, so the image did not show their faces.

The third image was far more damning. It showed Lucas moving through the pub area, the light from his phone shining almost at the camera and thus obscuring his features. Richard was also mostly obscured.

Montague, however, was a bit to the side, and his face showed up as clear as day.

"This is a problem," Lucas said.

"You are a master of understatement," Montague said. "Fortunately few of my friends would pick up a dirty little tabloid like this, and those that do for the comedic effect would not grass on me."

"You must have enemies in the magical community," Richard said.

"Many, but they would not injure their own position by talking to the police. I know a lot of dirty little secrets about a lot of people. Besides, if they got me arrested, the rest of the community would turn on them for ruining the best occult book business in London."

Lucas found one of the more annoying aspects of Montague's frequent boasts was that they were generally true.

"What about your neighbors?" Lucas asked.

"None would deign to read this rag sheet. I only picked it up because it was the most likely newspaper to carry the story. They just love any crime with a twist to it. You can rest assured that all the other cheap tabloids will pick it up for their evening editions."

"Nothing sells papers like a vampire," Richard said and sighed. "What does the article say?"

Montague put the paper down on the table, and they all read together.

"Last night, London's historic Highgate Cemetery and a neighboring pub were broken into by suspected Satanists."

"Satanists!" Richard growled. "Satan doesn't even exist."

"Funny the tabloid writers would believe in Satan when they most certainly don't believe in God," Montague quipped.

"Quiet," Lucas said. "I want to read this."

"Joe Thornton, landlord of The Red Lion pub on Highgate Hill Street, was awoken at around 11:45 p.m. last night by the sound of movement downstairs. He immediately called the police and then crept downstairs with a cricket bat."

"Well, that's a relief," Montague said. "In the dark, I mistook it for a machete."

"Only one of the burglars was in the main room when Mr. Thornton came downstairs, and the landlord only got a fleeting glimpse of an unusually tall and gaunt figure fleeing out the front door.

"'He looked like death warmed over,' the brave publican told the *Daily Mirror*. 'If he hadn't made such a racket, I could have sworn it was a ghost.'"

Richard snickered, and they continued to read.

"Suspecting that there were more intruders, Mr. Thornton crept down to the cellar, where he could see a faint light. There he saw that his beer kegs had been moved to reveal a portion of the wall that he had boarded up some years previously. The boarded space covered the entrance to an old Victorian tunnel leading to some early drainage works.

"'The Health and Safety inspectors told me to keep it sealed off, so I put up the board and stacked my beer kegs there to keep it out of sight. The intruders must have known it was down there.'"

"Nonsense," Montague scoffed. "It was as plain as day. He's just trying not to get fined.'"

"Mr. Thornton crept partway down the passage before he heard bloodcurdling screams echoing from the darkness.

"'It sounded like someone being sacrificed. I heard the sounds of something cutting through flesh, and the screams stopped. Then I heard maniacal laughter and chanting in what sounded like Latin. That's when I hurried back out of the tunnel, replaced the kegs, and waited for the police to come.'"

"What tosh," Lucas said.

"Police arrived within five minutes. The Red Lion's security system was found to have been turned off with the correct code. A routine check of the neighborhood turned up nothing, and the cemetery, which has been the site of many unseemly pranks, was found to be securely locked.

"It was only after studying local CCTV footage that the police found that the same motley group of people, pictured on page 5, that had broken into the pub had also picked the lock at the cemetery. The gang, who experts believe are a group of Satanists based in London, knew of a tunnel between the pub and a crypt in the cemetery. Both the crypt and the pub cellar have been sealed off and are being monitored with CCTV.

"The case calls to mind the famous Highgate Vampire mystery of 1970, almost fifty years ago to the day, when numerous sober and reliable witnesses spotted a tall, thin figure in a long black coat and top hat prowling through the burial ground. Leading paranormal investigators stated a vampire was loose in Highgate. Several graves were disturbed over the course of a few months, despite the cemetery being locked securely and closely watched. Later that year, the headless body of a woman, the flesh badly burnt, was found not far from the mausoleum that connects to The Red Lion.

"More shocking photos next page!"

Turning the page, they saw two more photos, one of the pub landlord standing by the opening into the tunnel and another of the tunnel itself. The caption read "Police cordoned off the tunnel and did not allow the *Daily Mirror* staff to investigate further. In a statement, the Met said that the tunnel leads directly to a mausoleum inside the cemetery and that the footprints of several people were found in the deep layer of dust on the floor. There is no evidence the graves were tampered with, but a padlock that secured the door was missing. The investigation continues."

Lucas sighed and leaned back in his chair. "Well, that complicates our lives."

"Mine more than yours," Montague said.

"What do we do?" Della asked.

"Keep looking for Autumn. What choice do we have?" Lucas asked.

The others nodded, but they looked as unhappy as Lucas felt.

Montague tapped the article. "It says the padlock to the mausoleum was missing. A spirit wouldn't have needed to remove it. That proves Autumn's kidnappers had been there before us."

"We all felt the spell they cast," Richard said then suddenly turned to the book dealer. "Wait. How did you know the code to the security system?"

"I know a chap who has tended bar at several of

the neighborhood pubs. He's added his own codes to the security systems and sells them to interested parties."

Lucas stared at him. "Why in the world would you want to know that?"

Montague shrugged and smiled. "It's simply another form of knowledge, and it did come in handy, didn't it?"

"Why did you have to punch in three codes?" Richard asked.

"Oh, in the stress of the situation, I bungled it. I couldn't remember it quite right. You can't expect me to know everything, my dusky friend, just most things."

"Doesn't your average security system go off if you get the code wrong three times?"

"It does indeed. Good thing I got it right the third time."

"So what do we do now?" Della asked.

"I have some other places we should check," Lucas said. "Other nexus points where they might use Autumn for a ritual."

The pained look on Della's face told him what she thought of that prospect.

"You can go back to Oxford, if you like," Lucas said gently.

Della hesitated for a second before shaking her head. "If I can help Autumn, I'll stay."

That warmed Lucas's heart. Autumn had ignored Della and had acted rudely toward her, and yet here Della was, risking her life to save her.

And Della's agreement, whether she admitted it to herself or not, was a tacit acknowledgement that her powers would come in handy.

It sure made Lucas feel better, having someone with that much innate Talent by his side. If she could learn to accept it and focus it, she could be more powerful than Richard.

"So where are you thinking we check next?" Richard asked. "There are so many spots."

For a moment, Lucas considered having Della run her hand across the map again, but opening an uninitiated person up to such a connection with the hidden world made her vulnerable, as they had learned all too well the previous evening. A spirit as powerful as Ebenezer King's might even be able to summon her and make her slip away from them and return to Highgate Cemetery.

Of course, with the police watching the place, she wouldn't end up back in the crypt. She'd end up in the local police station.

That would be almost as bad.

"I'm thinking of some of the spots near St. Paul's," Lucas said. "It's part of the ancient ritual center. A lot of the lines intersect there."

Montague cleared his throat. "I, um, think I'd better hold the fort here. I can do some research into this King fellow as well as royal blood rituals."

Lucas nodded. "With your face in the papers, it would be best if you stayed home for a day or two."

Yes, it would be best, but that's not the real reason you want to stay behind, is it?

You're scared.

Well, I suppose you have every right to be scared. If I was smart, I'd stay at home too.

11

ST. Bride's church lay at the end of a narrow lane just off Fleet Street. From Fleet Street, Della could look down a long road flanked by Victorian buildings of red brick uphill to the soaring white dome of St. Paul's cathedral, the iconic sight of the city's skyline. It was one of London's main tourist attractions, and the season being summer, there was a large crowd of people snapping photos in front of it.

But Lucas did not lead them there. Instead he led them down a deserted lane, at the end of which rose the slim spire of St. Bride's church, the top made of four circular sections, each smaller than the one below. It reminded Della of a wedding cake.

"How is it that in the most crowded neighborhood in the city, you can find a place with no people?" Della asked.

Lucas smiled. "In any other city, St. Bride's would be a star attraction. This close to St. Paul's, it's invisible."

"At least on the superficial level of perception," Richard said.

But not entirely forgotten. Once they passed down the lane, they came to a small churchyard. Three homeless men sat with their bundles on the tombstones, quietly drinking cheap cider from plastic two-liter bottles. Della could smell them ten feet off. The drinkers didn't even look at them as they passed through the heavy wooden door and entered the church.

Della's breath caught. The interior was beautiful. High arched windows of clear glass allowed the summer sun to bathe the interior with light, made brighter by the reflection off the whitewashed vaulted ceiling etched in gold and the marble floor. An altar draped with cloth of gold stood at one end beneath an ornate wooden arch held up by wooden Corinthian columns. Flanking this were pews of the same dark wood, providing an enclosed space that radiated warmth in contrast to the brilliance of the floor and ceiling.

"Beautiful," she whispered, temporarily forgetting her troubles. "Why don't they have stained-glass windows?"

"Got blasted to smithereens during the war," Lucas said. "The Luftwaffe did extensive remodeling in this part of town."

Richard stepped away from them to a side chapel. There, Della could see a small side altar covered in photographs. Richard lit a votive candle and put it on the row of others burning there. Then he stood for a moment in silence, facing the altar, before returning.

"Who are they?" Della asked, gesturing at the photos.

"Journalists who have died on duty. Back when Fleet Street was the center for publishing, before all the newspapers moved to lower-rent boroughs a few years ago, this was the journalists' church."

She looked at him quizzically. "You're a journalist?"

Richard smiled. "No, I'm a university administrator who casts spells in his spare time. But I have the greatest respect for all seekers of truth."

"This way," Lucas said.

He led them to a door at the far end of the church, where a staircase led down.

"The crypt?" Della asked.

"Yes," Lucas said. "Are you all right?"

"I'm fine." Della was surprised that she was. The memory of the crypt at Highgate still chilled her. But this place, somehow, with its bright interior and shrine to journalists, felt better. There were no dangers here. She felt sure of it.

Since when did feeling become more important than thinking? Della asked herself.

She had no answer to that.

They passed down a narrow set of stone steps to a brightly lit vaulted chamber. It was more of a narrow hallway, flanked by gravestones stacked against the wall. In front of the gravestones were the remains of a low stone wall of different make than the heavy blocks used in the church. It stood only up to her knees.

"This foundation looks medieval," Della said.

"Yes, it's from the eleventh-century church," Lucas said, "although the church has a much older history than that. It was said to have been founded by St. Bride of Ireland herself in the sixth century."

Della cocked her head. "I didn't know you studied medieval history."

"I don't. I read that information panel over

there," Lucas said with a grin, pointing at a sign behind her.

Della rolled her eyes. She had been hypnotized by some weirdo in a cemetery, chased by the police, had a fuzzy image of her committing criminal trespass appear in a cheap tabloid, and was wearing yesterday's clothes. The last thing she needed was Lucas being a smartass.

He motioned for her to follow. They walked along the passageway, a sign telling them that these gravestones had been gathered up after the Great Fire of London in 1666 destroyed the old St. Bride's church. Della noticed that many of the old stones were blackened with soot.

At the end of the passageway stood a low barrier made of Plexiglass. Della looked down and caught her breath. They stood over an excavated portion of the cellar about five feet by five feet. The bottom was covered with what could only have been Roman tile.

"This is what I wanted you to see," Lucas said.

"The church was built on a Roman house, by the looks of it," Della said. "Interesting, but I don't see what this has to do with Autumn or what happened last night."

Except that I have a weird feeling of calm here. That's all in my head, though. All this craziness is really getting to me. Maybe I feel calm because this place is so normal.

"It's more than that," Richard said. "When the archaeologists excavated this, they found evidence of Christian worship. This was probably a private home for Christians in the earliest days of Londinium, back in the reign of Claudius, when Christianity was still illegal. That probably makes St. Bride's the oldest house of Christian worship in the British Isles. It's a powerful spot and right on a nexus of ley lines."

"I thought you weren't Christian," Della said.

Richard shrugged. "Worship is worship."

"Why would the Christians build on a ley line? I thought that was pagan stuff."

"Because they are powerful. Ley lines are earth energy, and they have changed hands numerous times and have been used for various faiths, not to mention other purposes. Earth energy is more or less neutral and can be used by different people in different ways."

"So what's this got to do with Autumn?" As much as Della liked Richard, he was a lot like Lucas —too eager to believe anything, and he had a tendency to ramble off the point.

"This spot has been a center of worship since long before Christianity. Before the Romans came, the area was a center for Druidic rites going back as far as 1000 BC, maybe even earlier. It was one of the most important religious spots in England."

"Wait. I've read about the Celtic-Roman transition. This area was depopulated. There's no evidence for any settlement here before the Romans."

Lucas shook his head. "Richard's right. It was a major religious center. Hundreds if not thousands of people lived here."

"How could you know that without any evidence?"

Lucas and Richard glanced at each other. Della prepared herself for a fairy tale.

"It's a tradition handed down over many generations of practitioners," Lucas said. "Plus we've had confirmation from various spirits."

"Bloody hell," Della muttered.

"You're getting more English by the day," Lucas commented.

"Remember that you don't have to believe," Richard said, raising his hands in a calming gesture, "just as long as you understand that the people who took Autumn do believe. Before the Romans were here, the Druids were the chief religious authority in the land. Archaeologists don't know much about them because they didn't build in stone. They built in wood. And the tools they used in their rituals were also made of wood or leather. And of course, so many later phases of the city were built atop the old Celtic settlement. Very little has survived except for a few votive offerings thrown into the Thames, like the famous Battersea Shield. So we have to rely on other techniques than archaeology. Folklore is one I know you respect."

"Folklore evolves over time," Della said. "You can't go too far back with it."

"Bear with me. That hill that St. Paul's sits on is called Ludgate Hill. Now I'm sure you know Lud was an ancient Celtic king. According to Geoffrey of Monmouth's *History of the Kings of Britain*, he founded London and gave the city his name."

"Except Monmouth made up almost everything he wrote," Della said.

"A straight line west from here takes us to Parliament Hill, political center for the local Celtic tribes and now, of course, the political center for all the gibbering morons in office today. That's one ley line. Another heads farther east to the Tower of London, where once there stood a Celtic hill fort. There are more. Many more. The nexus here, which includes both St. Bride's and Ludgate Hill, has long been used for religious rituals. It's a powerful place. The nexus at Parliament Hill has served for millennia as a political center. The nexus at Highgate has been used since time immemorial for death rituals."

"I thought you said it only started as a cemetery in the 1830s."

"I said death ritual, not burial. And there may have been some of that in prehistoric times as well. London was a lot wetter back then than it is today. Several rivers used to flow through it that have been channels and covered over. Also, low areas have been drained. I bet the low area below Highgate was marshy ground. That's why the Victorians put some of the earliest drainage systems there, and they're still working today. The Celts may very well have used that marsh for human sacrifice. I wouldn't be at all surprised if when the present city expanded into that area, which I believe was in the sixteenth century, they found quite a few bog bodies like those that have been found in other ancient marshes across northern Europe. So we have ley lines tied with military authority linking up with those having to do with religion, which then link up with a nexus linked with political power, before moving on to a nexus for death rituals. These might all be connected in one vast ritual, with Autumn's royal blood being the sacrament."

Della found herself tuning out, as she so often did when her two weird friends rattled on about the occult, especially when they included hefty doses of pseudohistory. She turned and admired the Roman tiles. It was just a small section, not much bigger than a closet, excavated below the level of the medieval crypt. It appealed to her, though. She loved seeing these hidden bits of history. But what could any of this have to do with poor Autumn?

If there was only a more practical way to find her.

Della looked more closely at the tiles. It seemed there was something underneath, something hidden. She did not know how she could know this, and yet she felt it with as much certainty as she knew she was standing with two friends in a church crypt. Perhaps she should investigate further.

She knelt and placed the palms of her hands flat on the tile, not questioning how she could reach them from her vantage point behind the barrier.

The two-thousand-year-old tiles felt cool and brittle beneath her hands. A tingling went up her arms to wash over her entire body, and then she was no longer in the crypt.

She was somewhere else, somewhere very different.

Della stood on a narrow ledge at the edge of a tunnel some five feet wide and slightly higher. A swift stream flowed by, just inches from her feet. A little farther along the ledge, she saw the girl, the same girl she had seen the night before. The glow from her pure-white body illuminated the tunnel's interior. With a grave look on her face, the girl knelt and cupped her hands in the water. Then she rose and turned to Della, making an offering.

"No!"

The harsh word came growling out of the darkness behind her. Della whirled around and saw the tall man in the long black coat and top hat. His long, pale face twisted with rage, he grabbed Della by the shoulders and pulled her away.

12

DELLA COULDN'T STOP CRYING.

They sat in the pews in the side chapel dedicated to fallen journalists, Della sniffing softly into a handkerchief.

"I'm going crazy," she murmured, blowing her nose. "I'm going absolutely crazy."

Lucas had an arm around her, while Richard looked on sympathetically.

"You're not going crazy, Della," Lucas said in a quiet voice. "These things can be hard to accept."

"I thought that man in the mausoleum hypnotized me, or maybe even Montague. He's so strange. But neither of them are here!"

"Please keep your voice down," Richard said, looking around nervously.

Lucas felt eager to leave. They'd just committed another act of criminal trespass, after all, or at least Della had.

He nearly had a heart attack when he saw her hop the fence and kneel on the Roman tiles. Richard had been quicker to react. As soon as she started climbing over the barrier, he had placed his finger over the nearby CCTV camera. In a quiet church like this, no one was monitoring it, and by keeping the camera covered until they got her out of there, they hid any recording of her wrongdoing.

They couldn't hide the cracks in the ancient tiles that Della's feet left, though. Lucas decided not to tell her about that.

Neither of them had tried to stop her. Lucas had sensed this might be important and felt sure that Richard agreed.

Della shook her head. "I don't know what's come over me. I mean, I actually climbed over that fence and stood on some ancient tiles. I could have broken them!"

Lucas and Richard struggled hard to retain their poker faces.

"Thank you for pulling me out, Lucas," Della said.

Lucas's throat went dry. He had not pulled her

out, and neither had Richard. She had floated out. Actually floated. It looked like some strong, invisible hand had picked her up and put her back on the other side of the barrier, right between Richard and Lucas. The temperature had plunged to almost arctic levels for a minute. Thankfully, no one else had been visiting the crypt at that moment. That would have been awkward.

"What am I going to do?" she moaned. "I should see a shrink or something."

"Or maybe you should start accepting the evidence of your own senses," Lucas said.

Della shook her head.

Richard put a hand on her arm. "But what about what happened with your advisor and Keaton Whitaker? You yourself had to battle a spirit and—"

"Stop!" Della cried.

A youthful minister in flowing black vestments came around the corner and stared. He had obviously been waiting just out of sight, worried about the crying girl flanked by two men.

Della looked up at him. "Sorry," she sniffled. "These are my friends."

"You sure you're all right?" the minister asked.

"No. I mean yes. Thank you."

"If you feel in need of spiritual counseling, I'll be over by the altar."

The minister left, glancing once over his shoulder to fix the two men with a suspicious stare.

"Let's get out of here," Richard whispered. He nudged Della. "I've never seen a minister that young. Liked the robes too. Very swish. Maybe I should go get some spiritual counseling."

Della managed a smile and wiped her eyes.

"Yeah, let's get out of here. I think I've embarrassed myself enough for one day."

You haven't embarrassed yourself, Della. You've merely started breaking down your concept of reality, Lucas thought.

Or something else is trying to.

They left and went to a nearby cafe to have a cup of tea.

"This actually tells us a lot," Richard said once they had sat down at a corner table away from a crowd of loud German tourists. "You sure it was the same two figures?"

Della nodded, not looking at him.

"Then they are traveling down the ley lines. That means the lines have been opened up. The ritual is at least partially complete."

"What do you mean?" Della asked, sounding

annoyed. Lucas suspected she was getting to the end of her tolerance.

But you're nowhere near the end of your journey, I'm afraid.

Richard went on.

"Imagine building a circuit. First you connect the wires to whatever you want to light up, and then you connect it to a power source. The ley lines are the wires, and the Earth energy is the power source. These two spirits act as the electric current."

"So what's it supposed to light up?" Della asked.

Richard sighed. "I'm not sure about that yet."

Della paused for a moment, looking into the dark depths of her tea. Then, in a quiet voice, she said, "I remember everything now. Everything from last night in Highgate."

She took a deep breath and told them the whole story, from the moment she felt that strange pull to walk along a certain path in the cemetery to when they ran away and she turned to see the tall figure, no doubt Ebenezer King, leering at her through the fence. She continued by telling, in all the detail she could remember, what she had seen just then in the crypt of St. Bride's church.

When she finished, the three of them sat in silence for a moment, absorbing the enormity of it all.

Della's eyes welled up again. No doubt she was beginning to believe.

And it was wrecking the fragile world she had constructed for herself.

Lucas's heart went out to her. If Richard hadn't been there, he would have taken her in his arms and told her everything would be all right. He might have even done more than that.

But he didn't, and the moment he thought it, he knew he wouldn't. Not because of Richard sitting across from him but simply because he didn't have the guts.

He cleared his throat and said, "You mentioned you saw an underground stream."

"More like a small river. The water moved pretty fast. I got the impression that it was under the church's crypt."

"Do you know about the River Fleet?"

"No."

Lucas and Richard glanced at each other.

"That's what you saw," Richard said. "It's an old river, one of many that have been covered over and hidden in modern London. Fleet Street gets its name from it. The river flows almost right underneath where we're sitting now. St. Bride's was located on its banks."

"Why would they cover over a river?" Della said.

"Because by the eighteenth century, it had become a stinking rubbish dump, an open sewer that was considered the filthiest body of water in London, and that was quite an accomplishment. It was covered over sometime in the late 1700s. I'm not sure exactly when."

"Why would that girl have been offering me water from it?" Della asked. It sounded like she had to practically force the words out of her mouth. Even saying them was an admission that she was considering the reality of her vision. The pained look on her face filled Lucas with pity.

He hadn't wanted to believe, either, even though he knew the spirit world was all too real.

How couldn't he know? When he was a child, his parents had been snatched from him by malignant spirits right in front of his eyes.

Unlike Della, who didn't believe, Lucas had believed all his life and desperately tried not to.

"I don't know why Cordelia's spirit would do that," Richard said in answer to Della's question. He glanced at Lucas. "But I think I know who could tell us."

Bloody hell.

He means Cassandra.

Lucas shifted in his seat and grimaced.

"I don't think she'd want to help," he said.

"Who?" Della asked.

"She's an expert on London psychogeography, especially its hidden waterways and associated rituals," Richard said. "You know that."

"Who?" Della asked.

"She wouldn't help me. Not in a million years."

"We need her. I'm sure if we explained—"

"*Who?*"

Lucas and Richard looked at Della, as did everyone else in the cafe. She blushed, aware her outburst had brought too much attention. Lucas had never seen her like this before.

"Cassandra Blakely," he said, the name coming out as a grunt.

Della frowned, no doubt sensing something.

"A practitioner," Richard interjected. "She's lived in central London all her life and knows all its ritual spaces. I'm afraid we're a bit out of my area of expertise. And Lucas, while he has the Talent, has neglected his studies. Montague knows this area well but can't really leave the house at the moment."

Not that he would want to if he could, the coward, Lucas added silently.

Della looked at Lucas then Richard and back again.

"So what's wrong with her?"

"Lucas and Cassandra have a bit of a..."

"History," Lucas mumbled.

Della arched an eyebrow. "History?"

"Ancient history."

Della leaned forward and frowned. "I love ancient history. Do tell."

"This is the only kind of ancient history you won't be interested in," Lucas assured her.

I'm not interested in it, either, but it sure is interested in me.

13

IF DELLA HADN'T THOUGHT MUCH of Autumn, she automatically hated Cassandra.

This woman was arrogant and rude, obviously disliked Della at first sight, and didn't even have the benefit of having been kidnapped to soften Della's feelings toward her.

It didn't help that she was drop-dead gorgeous.

It also didn't help that she somehow remained drop-dead gorgeous as she led them through a sewer. The leggy brunette with the pert nose and sparkling green eyes would look good anywhere.

Cassandra Blakely worked as an engineer for Thames Water, so it was easy for her to make some excuse to get them all down under Fleet Street, equipped with waders, reflective vests, and hard hats equipped with powerful electric lights.

And surgical masks. The surgical masks were essential.

They had entered an open drain under Blackfriars Bridge, and now they sloshed thigh deep through murky water that chilled them through the watertight rubber of their waders. Unidentifiable objects floated past them or stuck to the two-hundred-year-old brick walls. Actually, if Della had focused on them, she could probably identify them, but that was too much for her mind to stand right now. The possibility of magic actually existing had already overloaded her.

"I really don't know why a water spirit would pick her," Cassandra said to Lucas as they led their small party through the muck. "She doesn't seem up to the task."

Lucas had told her everything, much to Della's embarrassment. It was like he was telling a complete stranger she was insane. Casandra had taken it all very seriously, though, and had even managed a sympathetic look or two.

"She's got a great deal of innate Talent," Lucas objected.

"I sense that, obviously. It's just that I can't see

her ever putting it to good use. She's even worse than you."

It had been like this since Cassandra had met them at the cafe. She had been talking about Della as if she wasn't there. Lucas had fallen into it too. And the way Cassandra cozied up to him left Della fuming.

Della tried to focus on what lay ahead. Their headlamps shone bright down the tunnel, revealing nothing but a featureless straight passage of brick a third filled with icky water. Richard sloshed next to her, looking behind them every few steps as if worried something might be following.

Della appreciated the sentiment. This was a creepy place, so silent and hidden compared to the blaring city above, but her gut told her the danger lay ahead, not behind.

"Where are you taking us?" Della asked.

Instead of replying to her, Cassandra addressed Lucas.

"The River Fleet has been channeled somewhat off its original course. We're coming to a stretch up ahead where it does follow the ancient line. At that point, we'll actually be following one of the city's many ley lines, and we'll be passing right by St. Bridget's Well."

"Don't you mean St. Bride's?" Della asked.

"Trust an academic to miss the obvious," Cassandra said with an exaggerated groan. "Bride is a linguistic corruption of Bridget, and Bridget is an old pagan goddess of—"

"The spring, I know," Della snapped.

"And creativity and healing and fertility and all beginnings," Cassandra said, counting off the list on her fingers with noticeable impatience. "You're lucky that water spirit was offering you a drink from it. It's been dry on this plane of existence for two hundred years."

"From my vision, it looked like she was offering me water from the river," Della said.

I can't believe I'm taking this seriously. But what can I do? It's not like the world is giving me a choice.

"You must have been mistaken," Cassandra said. "The River Fleet has no magical attributes. It's the sacred wells along its banks that have the real power."

"Does this river flow beneath Highgate Cemetery too?"

Cassandra's laugh echoed down the tunnel, making Della cringe.

"Typical Yank. Doesn't even know where she is!"

"The spirit offered her a drink from the water

beneath Highgate too," Richard said, speaking for the first time in a while. He had been mostly silent ever since Cassandra showed up. Della got the feeling Richard didn't like her any more than she did.

Cassandra nodded, the beam from her hard hat wavering over the water. "I must admit that confused me."

Cassandra stumbled, and Lucas caught her.

"Oh, thank you. You've always been such a gentleman," she said, hanging on him. Della got the distinct impression that fall had been fake. Too bad it hadn't turned into a real one. The snob might have fallen headfirst into this filthy water. That would have brightened Della's day.

Lucas detached himself, not without some difficulty, and Cassandra turned back to face Della, shining her headlamp right in Della's eyes. Della looked away, annoyed. She hated people getting into her personal space.

"Did Lucas ever talk about me?" Cassandra asked.

"No." Della didn't realize she could put so much anger and contempt into a single word.

"Oh, I suppose that's not surprising. You don't talk about old conquests with new ones."

"Cassandra!" Lucas shouted.

"Do keep your voice down," Cassandra said without looking back at him. "Who knows what lurks down here."

"We're not dating," Della growled.

"Just sleeping together? Yes, that's more Lucas's style."

Della flushed despite the clammy tunnel. She would have loved to have come up with a witty, biting comeback. She would have loved to be the kind of person capable of doing that, but she wasn't. Faced with Cassandra's form of verbal bullying, she always retreated into her shell. This was probably, Della mused, why people like Cassandra picked on her so much. Story of her life.

She tried to tune out as Cassandra led them down the tunnel, continuing to relate how she and Lucas had met when they were only eighteen and had a whirlwind love affair. Lucas cut her off just as she started getting detailed about sexual positions.

Cassandra giggled and finally fell silent.

"It stinks in here," Della grumbled.

It was meant as a double entendre, but no one got it.

"The River Fleet stopped being a sewer two centuries ago," Lucas said, "but with the amount of trash thrown on the streets of London every day, some of it is bound to make it down here."

It was supposed to have been an insult to your ex-girlfriend, Della seethed. *Thanks for undercutting it. You probably did that on purpose.*

"We're getting there," Richard whispered.

It wasn't until he said it that Della noticed that the tunnel had been getting progressively colder. That beautiful bully had distracted her. The tunnel jagged at an angle. Della thought it was turning north but couldn't be sure. It was so disorienting down here.

"Yes, we are getting there," Cassandra said softly. She edged behind Lucas, and this time it seemed that she wasn't trying to bait Della. She was actually scared. That got Della scared too. "This doesn't feel right."

"What do you mean?" Lucas asked.

Cassandra stood right behind Lucas now, her hands gripping his broad shoulders.

"I've been down here before. Many times. You know how much I've explored London's waterways. I've never felt it like this before."

"We've come to the part that aligns with the ley line, haven't we?" Lucas asked.

She squeezed his shoulders. "You're always so

sensitive, my dear, even when you don't want to be. Yes, we are walking along the ley line. But instead of the pure energy that's usually here, I'm sensing a lot of negative energy, tainted energy."

So am I, Della thought. *From you.*

"That ritual they did in Highgate must have sullied the entire ley line," Richard said.

They moved ahead more slowly. In the distance, on the left-hand wall, they saw a break in the brickwork about halfway up, a little side channel only a couple of feet wide.

"That's the conduit to St. Bridget's Well," Della said. She didn't know how she could be so sure, only that she was.

Cassandra glanced over her shoulder at her.

"My my, the little American does have the Talent after all."

They came to it, the chill growing greater.

"We should leave," Richard said.

"In a minute," Cassandra said. She turned again to Della. "Is this the place you saw in your vision?"

She shined her headlamp down the side channel. It angled up a bit then went straight to a little round hollow beneath a vertical shaft. Although the entire section was damp, they could see no pooled or flowing water.

"This was the well," Cassandra explained. "The River Fleet has been channeled and broken up so much that the water level never gets up to the well anymore. We're right beneath the churchyard. The top of the well stood right beside it. Did the girl you saw bring you down there?"

Della frowned. "No, it was the river. I told you."

"Why would a water spirit want you to drink from the river? It makes no sense," Cassandra said. "Try to think."

"I *am* thinking," Della said, frustrated. She was finally beginning to admit there might be something to all this craziness, and now no one believed her? "Like I told you, the girl offered me a drink from the river, and that creepy old man, the one Lucas and Richard think is buried in the crypt at Highgate, shouted, 'No,' and pulled me away from her."

Cassandra looked around, confused. "It makes no sense."

And then suddenly Cassandra wasn't there anymore. She shot straight down into the water with a splash, a large wake rippling down the tunnel both ways.

"Cassandra!" Lucas shouted, reaching into the water where she had disappeared.

Lucas launched backward, slamming into the

brick wall of the underground channel with a grunt. He slipped into the water, flailing around and barely able to keep from going under.

While Richard helped his friend, Della surged forward to where Cassandra had vanished. A biting chill ran through her body, nearly paralyzing her. She gritted her teeth and plunged her arms into the water, feeling around for Cassandra.

An invisible force hit her in the chest like a hammer. She felt herself fly back.

"No!" she shouted.

The force dissipated, and she found that unlike Lucas, who was still sputtering and stunned in Richard's arms, she had only flown back a couple of feet and remained standing.

Willpower, she realized. *It's all about willpower, just like when I pushed out that intruder in my apartment.*

Intruder? Demon!

There are no demons. That's impossible.

Della didn't have time for an existential crisis right now. Something was trying to kill them. That much was for sure. Cassandra wouldn't be able to hold her breath for much longer.

She waded through the water, having to use all her strength to move forward, as if the water was made of half-dried concrete. Richard was chanting something, but Della did not look in his direction. Instead she focused on pushing through the resistance that strengthened around her. She got to the spot where Cassandra had been pulled under the surface, took a deep breath, and dove down.

She had closed her eyes to keep the filthy water from touching them. It was doubtful she would have been able to see anything in the murky water in any case. With fingers chilled to near numbness, she groped around, and her hand finally clasped an ankle. She brought her other hand down and grabbed Cassandra's leg. The woman was struggling, fighting for her life against whatever had ahold of her. Della moved up her body to find her arm and got a good grip.

Della planted her feet and stood, hauling up Cassandra like an oversized fish.

They broke the surface at the same time, sputtering and coughing. Cassandra made horrible choking sounds. Della wiped her eyes just in time to see her puke into the water.

Must have gotten a mouthful of the stuff, Della thought.

The delight she took in that felt unwarranted.

Della cast around. She didn't see anything in the

water. What had grabbed Cassandra and pushed her and Lucas?

The two men waded to them, Lucas grabbing Cassandra as she doubled over from nausea and almost fell back below the surface again. Della felt a spike of jealousy as they soothed her and made sympathetic noises.

Base emotions quickly got pushed aside, and she felt something cold coil around her ankle. It yanked on her, pulling her off balance. Della grabbed onto the brick wall, scraping her fingers and splitting her nails, and summoned up as much willpower as she could. The thing slid away, feeling like an icy serpent.

She turned to the others, trembling with cold and fear.

"It's like a snake. It's—"

She felt something coil around her neck and yank her beneath the surface.

She banged against the bottom of the channel, the pressure on her neck tightening. Della flailed and struggled, clawing at her neck. Even though she could feel the thing pressing against her throat and choking her, her hands passed through only water.

Her entire body began to shake from cold—all except her lungs, which burned for lack of oxygen.

The thing had caught her midsentence, when she was breathing out, and she had little air left to spare.

Something bumped into her, something that felt human. Solid and male. Lucas? She reached for him, but he was gone.

This thing is throwing them back, keeping them away until I suffocate.

She spread out her arms and legs and couldn't feel anything. The three of them must be trying to help her, but they couldn't get close.

Her thoughts became muddled. The lack of oxygen was pulling her down into unconsciousness.

I'm going to get killed by something I don't even believe in. I'll die in a sewer before I even get to live my life.

Then something her father had said to her rang through her mind. It had been on the night before she left for England for her first year at Oxford.

Della, I know you're nervous. I know you're scared. This is the first time you'll live away from home, and you're flying across an entire ocean. New people, a new country, and new challenges. So all the old fears are coming back up. You've gone from someone who got flustered speaking to a waitress to a straight-A student who gives academic papers at meetings of the Archaeological Institute of America.

You're a state champion fencer. You've taken your fear and turned it into determination.

Just keep doing that.

Della focused. With the last scraps of consciousness, she honed her mind into a single sharp thrust of will, like a powerful lunge that scores the winning point in a fencing tournament.

She snapped into a seated position, the cold coil around her neck vanishing. She got her legs underneath her and pushed off, shooting out of the water to gasp for air. Before she even had a chance to get her balance and wipe her eyes, her attacker slammed into her and knocked her into the water again.

Hands like claws, Della grabbed at the thing wrapping itself around her body like some invisible python. She willed it to be solid, willed it to be something she could grab ahold of.

And it became so, became a slick, slimy length of coldness that she tore at, ripping and shredding until it fell apart in her hands.

14

BY THE TIME Lucas was able to get to Della and pull her out of the water without anything trying to toss him around, she was half-dead. He gave her a squeeze around the middle that made her eject a stream of water and vomit.

"It's gone," Richard said. "She banished it."

There was relief in his words—and wonder.

"You're right," Cassandra replied, eyes wide with fear. "The chill has gone."

"I feel half-frozen," Lucas said, dragging Della along as they made their way to the entrance. They were all soaked to the skin. That entity had given them all a good dunking.

"Yes, but the ambient temperature has risen.

Whatever that was has gone back to its own plane of existence," Richard said.

They sloshed along in the half darkness. Only Lucas's headlamp had survived the fight, flickering every now and then through its cracked lens. They were made to be water-resistant, but they weren't made to be slammed against brick walls and held under water for extended periods of time by supernatural entities.

"What was that?" Della groaned.

"A water weird," Cassandra said. "A magical creature summoned using water magic. Quite a powerful one." She stared at Della in amazement. "And despite having no training, you banished it back to its own plane of existence."

"Things like that don't exist," Della said, coughing again. "How can this be happening?"

She looked on the point of tears. Lucas gave her a reassuring hug. He caught Cassandra frowning at her and tried not to care.

But he did.

Cassandra wasn't an easy person to dismiss.

After a miserable taxi ride to Cassandra's flat, which cost three times the usual price because they all stank and dripped on the seats, they took turns taking a much-needed shower and stuffed their clothes into the washing machine. Cassandra was subdued, with none of her usual banter. She lent Della some clothes, all of which were too big for her, and Della sat on the sofa, looking rumpled as she stared into space and said nothing. Richard and Lucas had nothing to wear except towels and blankets until Cassandra produced one of Lucas's old sweaters.

"I wondered where that went," Lucas said with a rueful smile. "I thought I'd lost it."

"A keepsake," Cassandra said. "I suppose you'll take it now."

She went to fix some tea as they all sat, tired and unkempt, in Cassandra's living room.

"That was a close one," Richard said after a long silence. "We nearly all died."

"Whoever kidnapped your friend has opened up the ley lines to some very powerful magic," Cassandra said, coming out of the kitchen with the tea. They each took a cup and drank gratefully.

No one spoke again until she made a second cup. Lucas felt utterly exhausted, and Della looked emotionally numb. He would have sat next to her, but she had chosen an armchair pulled a little away from the circle made by the sofa and two other chairs. Lucas suspected that if they were back in

Oxford, she would have left for her own flat already, and he wouldn't have seen her again for days.

"The question remains," Lucas said, "what exactly are they trying to do?"

Cassandra shrugged. "I don't know much about the magic of royal bloodlines. Water magic and the ley network of London are my remit. Whatever they're doing, they know we're onto them, and they've set up defenses. What's interesting is that there seems to be a fight going on at a higher level. That girl, the water spirit that Della saw, is obviously trying to help but is being stopped by the spirit of Ebenezer King."

Lucas nodded. "They must have summoned him as a sort of spiritual mercenary. Montague James is researching him now."

"With that library, he's sure to find out something," Cassandra said then smiled. "I must say, Lucas, you certainly know how to show a lady an interesting time."

"We're still no closer to finding Autumn," Della said.

Lucas thought for a moment. "I think we might be. We have a general idea of what they're doing. With a little more background on the spirit they raised in Highgate, we might be able to anticipate their next move."

Cassandra had some food delivered, and they ate as their clothes finished washing. Once Cassandra had put their clothes through the dryer and they could get dressed again, Lucas stood up.

"We should get back and discuss this with Montague."

"He's not much help," Richard said. "We could have used his Talent down in the River Fleet. Maybe we wouldn't have gotten such a dunking."

"He has knowledge and contacts and a free place to stay in London," Lucas said.

Richard made a face. "Listen, I took a personal day yesterday, and I called in for another this morning. After this, I'll have to get a note from the NHS. I'm going to have to go back to Oxford this afternoon and go to my local clinic with some story. If I get a note from a clinic here, my manager will ask questions."

"We need you," Della said, looking worried.

"I know, and I will be back. But sadly, even when you're hunting practitioners of black magic and the spirits of dead occultists, sometimes the office job gets in the way."

Della handed over her keys. "Do you remember where I live?"

"Yes."

"Go get me some more clothes and the toiletries in my bathroom. I have a feeling we're going to be down in London for a while."

Richard smiled. "Glad to have you on the team."

He left. Lucas and Della decided to head back to Montague's place.

Just as they were going down the stairs of Cassandra's building, Lucas's ex-girlfriend called to Della to come back.

"You mentioned you needed something from your house. I have some spare toiletries you can borrow and a book I think you should read."

Della went back up the stairs and disappeared back into Cassandra's flat. Lucas stood uncertainly on the landing. After a minute, he checked his phone. They had fortunately left all their phones in Cassandra's car before exploring the River Fleet, so they had all survived. No calls from Montague. A text from Aunt Mary asking how things were going. He'd call her later. He put the phone back into his pocket. After another minute, he checked the time. What was taking those two so long?

He glanced up the stairway at the open door to Cassandra's flat. He could hear them talking in there but couldn't make out the words. Should he go back up?

Lucas checked his phone again. Three minutes. Della had been up there for three whole minutes. How long did it take to grab a book and some bathroom things? What was Cassandra doing? Giving her makeup tips?

More like she was talking about him.

That decided it. He should get up there. Cassandra had always been pushy and possessive. It was one of the reasons he had cut it off. Who knew what she was saying to Della up there?

Just as he put his foot on the first step, they came out the door. Lucas quickly pulled back to stand where he was before.

"Thank you," Della said. She was clutching a large plastic supermarket bag. "I'll keep it in mind."

Della walked down the stairs to him. Cassandra locked eyes with Lucas and gave him a smile before closing the door.

What was that supposed to mean? What kind of smile had that been? He wasn't sure. It hadn't been the kind of honest, open smile of one friend to another. No chance of that with her. Had it been a mocking smile? Perhaps. More like a mischievous smile, and Cassandra could certainly be mischievous.

Good Lord, what was she up to?

"Keep what in mind?" Lucas asked as they left the building.

Della looked at him askance. "Nothing."

Lucas resisted the urge to ask again. That would only make him look desperate. They walked down the sidewalk in the late-afternoon pedestrian rush.

"What book did she lend you?" he asked, changing tack.

Della rummaged through a collection of shampoo, disposable razors, and various other feminine bric-a-brac and pulled out a thick paperback.

"*An Introduction to Neo-Antiquarianism.* I've read this. A good basic primer." He studied her. "Are you going to read it?"

They came to a bus stop.

"Yeah," Della said and sighed. "I don't know how much of this stuff I believe, but something sure is going on. I've never had anything weird happen to me in my whole life, and now two crazy cults have come out of the woodwork in a single summer. I have a feeling this is going to happen again."

"Sorry for dragging you into all of this."

"It's not your fault." Della looked tired as she sat

down on the bench at the bus stop. A few other people stood or sat nearby, oblivious in their own conversations or the music on their headphones. No one suspected the nature of what they were talking about. How could they? The other people lived normal lives, worrying about normal things. Lucas had always wanted a life like that. He had tried very hard to cultivate that life.

The hidden world obviously had other plans.

"Why did she give you all those things? Richard is going to fetch your own."

Della managed a ghost of a smile. "She said, 'Never trust a man to provide what a woman needs.'"

Oh, fantastic.

"I think you need to read that book," Lucas said.

"I will. Hopefully I won't have to bang it against the head of a kidnapper. I bent the spine of one of them on his forehead."

Suddenly Lucas remembered something.

"What was that book you bought the other day?"

"You mean the early archaeological journal?"

"No, the other one."

"An old book titled *Medieval German Kingdoms.* It was from the 1920s."

Lucas's jaw dropped. "Why did you buy that?"

"I... I'm not sure. It's not really my specialty. I do

more prehistoric stuff." Her brow furrowed. "That's strange. Why would I pay forty pounds for a book on a subject I don't study?"

"Because you had a moment of psychic foreshadowing. That's why."

"Oh, come on."

"Autumn's bloodline is from the Principality of Anhalt, a medieval German kingdom."

Della rubbed her temples and swore.

"Text Richard and tell him to bring it," Lucas said. "Anything about royalty in the archaeological journal?"

"No." Della's answer came out relieved, almost defiant.

Keep it together, Della, Lucas thought. *We need you more than you could ever imagine.*

When they got back to Montague's place, he didn't answer the doorbell. Lucas called him, and he answered on the second ring. It turned out he was at home after all.

"Sorry," the bookseller said, peeking out the door to study every corner of the square. "I'm worried someone might be coming for me."

Then he noticed the state the two of them were in.

"Good Lord, what happened to you? Della, you have bruises all around your neck!"

Lucas looked at her. What had been red marks a while before had turned into livid purple bruises.

Della touched her neck, fumbled through the shopping bag, and produced a long pink scarf, which she draped around her neck.

"Cassandra warned me it was getting bad. I've been in such a muddle her words just passed through my head."

"You met Cassandra?" Montague asked as he urged them inside and closed the door behind them. "I'm doubly glad I didn't go out with you today."

He locked the door, put on a chain, and slid two bolts. They sat down in his living room and explained everything they had experienced. Montague listened in silence, his face growing increasingly concerned. Once they finished, the book dealer shook his head.

"Cassandra was overpowered by a water spirit? These people are powerful. She's so attuned to that sort of magic she should have been able to break that spell with barely a thought. But it was you, Della, who managed the job. You have quite a bit of Talent."

Della slumped. "I think I'm going to have a nap."

"Just a moment, and then you can have a well-earned rest. I need to tell you what I've learned about your old chum Ebenezer King."

Della groaned. "Make it quick, please."

"Very well. As we've mentioned, King was a major figure in occult circles in the early nineteenth century. He had quite the maleficent reputation. I've discovered that he was also one of the original subscribers to the Highgate Cemetery project."

"Subscribers?" Della asked.

"The money was raised by subscription. People donated a certain sum and got a plot in return. King donated quite a lot and was gifted with enough room for a mausoleum."

"One right over the tunnels," Lucas said.

"Indeed. He chose his spot well. I've also found a bit about that wife of his. A poor girl from an unknown family. She was fourteen when they got married."

Della frowned. "Ew."

"That wasn't all that uncommon in those days. Girls were considered financial burdens and were married as soon as they reached puberty and a suitable groom could be found."

"Who would think of Ebenezer King as suitable?" Della asked. "He looks like a psychopath."

"And his reputation was foul even back then. He had money, though, and money was one thing Cordelia's family certainly lacked. I could find no record of her. I phoned a genealogist friend at the national archives, and he could find no record of her either. Birth records were a bit sketchy for the poorer folk in those days, and no respectable family would have given their daughter to such a man. My friend did find the birth records for Ebenezer. He was born right here in London to an upper-middle-class family in 1798."

"The grave said he was never born and was just passing through this material plane," Della said.

"Oh, that's just a bit of show business," Montague said with a chuckle. "Lots of occultists use that phrase. I've even heard modern Indian gurus use the exact same words. An effort to make them appear more impressive than they actually are."

"But Ebenezer King really was impressive," Lucas said. "He was the real item."

"Hmm, quite. What interested me was the date of their death. Both died on December 31, 1839, the last day of the year that Highgate Cemetery opened. Theirs must have been one of the very first graves to be installed, if not the first."

"How did they die?" Lucas asked.

"The official records list 'misadventure,' which tells us absolutely nothing. Newspaper reports at the time tell breathless tales of demon summonings and the two being found burnt to a crisp in their house, with nothing else in the room so much as scorched. There was quite the media flap about it. All the stories contradict each other, however, and occasionally even contradict themselves. It's difficult to tease out any truth from them. All agree, however, that two bodies were found and were so badly burned they could only be identified by their wedding rings. The occult tradition here is a bit more fruitful. Certain works in my possession tell a more believable and far grislier tale."

"If this involves Cordelia being a virgin sacrifice, I don't want to hear about it," Della said. She had slumped farther in her seat, and her eyes had screwed shut.

"No, nothing like that. It appears that Ebenezer made her participate in rituals but not in that manner."

"Poor girl. She must have been terrified. She looked so nice and innocent."

"She didn't get to remain so, unfortunately," Montague said. "She was forced to help him. According to tradition handed down by some associates of Ebenezer's, he got involved with Charles Bedford, a bastard son of the Duke of Bedford. Charles was given a remittance to stay quiet about his parentage and spelled his name Beauford. Having nothing to do and a lot of money to do it with, he fell into a bad circle and ended up in the darkest of the dark arts. Being wealthy, he was attractive to the occultist, but there was something more that attracted Ebenezer."

"Royal blood?" Della asked.

Montague cocked his head. "You really are psychic, aren't you?"

"No, it's just that the English aristocracy is horribly inbred."

"True enough. The Duke of Bedford was a nephew of the king, and so Charles also had royal blood in him. And we have proof that they used it in rituals. Here."

Montague produced a volume that looked privately printed. The pages were all photocopies of various documents. He opened to a page showing a handwritten letter and put his finger on the top line.

"This is a letter from Ebenezer to one of his associates. Right here it says, 'Have made a golden chalice and bring it to the winter solstice ritual. Make sure it is properly cleansed and prepared to receive the sanctified blood of Albion.' That means English royal blood. You can see Ebenezer's signature at the bottom."

Della studied the letter.

"This is a woman's handwriting."

Lucas leaned in. "Are you sure?"

"It certainly looks like it."

"Hmm," Montague said. "I think you're right. Ebenezer must have been using poor Cordelia as his personal secretary. I think our kidnappers raised the spirit of Ebenezer because they wanted someone associated with royal blood magic, someone who had done it before."

Della suddenly raised her hands. "I'm done."

Montague turned to her. "I beg your pardon?"

"I'm done," she said brusquely. "I'm going to sleep. Stay here and talk if you want to."

Della rose and moved for the stairs. Montague was about to object when Lucas raised a cautionary hand. He had seen her like this before. The poor woman was overwhelmed. She needed silence and solitude. She had experienced more than her mind and body could bear, and she needed to hide within herself.

Lucas knew all about that. He'd been struggling with the same situation his entire life.

15

DELLA LOCKED HER BEDROOM DOOR, put the chair and glass against it for extra security, and stood motionless for a second in utter exhaustion.

She dropped the shopping bag with a clatter. It had been nice of Cassandra to lend her those things, a gesture of goodwill after how catty she had been. Her whole attitude had changed after the fight beneath London.

What hadn't been so nice was what Cassandra had said about Lucas.

"He was hurt badly at a young age. That's made him selfish. Be careful, Della. You won't be able to change him. I failed, and I suspect I'm a lot better at manipulating men than you are."

Cassandra hadn't even asked if Della was interested in him. She had simply assumed.

Then Cassandra had given her that book.

"You look the bookish type. That's good, because you have a lot of reading ahead of you. Start with this. It's not all true, but enough of it is that you'll begin to see what you've stepped into."

Visions of spirits... hidden lines of Earth energy... snakes made of water...

Moving over to the small mirror set atop the bureau, Della removed the scarf from around her neck and studied the bruise. Yes, here was tangible proof that it had all happened. She pressed the area with her fingertips and winced. It was tender. Lifting her shirt, she found bruises on her side too. Her fingers were all raw as well, with several nails chipped or broken. She always kept them trimmed close for fieldwork, but even so, they had been badly banged up.

She could think of no way this could have happened within the parameters of the world she knew. The only rational explanation was that there was no rational explanation.

It could still be hypnosis. They could have put these marks on you while you were under mental control.

Della dug her fingers into the bruise until she hissed with pain.

This is real. Deal with it. Lucas and Richard would have never done this. Cassandra maybe, but they wouldn't have let her.

Della flopped down onto the bed and lay there a long time, the events of the day crowding into her head, brilliant and painful like a stained-glass window exploding in her face. Finally, fatigue pulled her under, and she slept.

By the time she awoke, the evening was well advanced, and the golden light of summer sunset filtered through the blinds. The soft colors should have cheered her, but since they heralded the approach of night, they only filled her with dread.

She supposed Montague and Lucas were still down there talking, planning. Perhaps Cassandra had come over too. Richard would have made it back to Oxford and gone to the clinic with some excuse. He would be back down again sometime tonight or early tomorrow morning. She wondered if he had found anything significant in that book she had bought.

Della groaned and turned over, pulling the blanket over her head. It was hot and stuffy beneath it, but she didn't care. It blocked out the world. Let someone else deal with it for a while.

As much as she tried, she couldn't get back to sleep. The memories of the cemetery and the underground river came back to her. Rational explanations were tried and rejected. Alternative explanations made no sense.

A soft knock at the door. Della jumped, letting out a little yelp. Peeking from beneath her covers, she noticed that the sunlight had dimmed noticeably.

Lucas's quiet voice called out, "Della, are you all right?"

She lay there, tense and silent.

Another soft knock. "Della?"

Silence. After a minute, she heard the sound of receding footsteps.

She let out a long breath of relief.

Just leave me alone. All I want is to be left alone.

Then another thought overwhelmed that.

Alone and hiding beneath the covers like some frightened kid? Fat lot of good you'll be to Autumn like this. You need to get out there and help.

Help how? I don't even know what's going on. None of this makes any sense.

Well, how the hell do you know what makes sense or not? You were basically a shut-in through most of your childhood and then hid behind books and a fencing mask. You don't know anything about the real world. You hide from it.

I know that ghosts and water spirits aren't supposed to exist.

Yeah, well, they do. Time to level up.

It took another fifteen minutes of fighting with herself to get out of bed and another ten minutes to actually leave the room.

She went downstairs to find Lucas and Montague at the table in the study, scrutinizing several newspapers and drinking more cups of tea.

Montague looked up from the papers. "You're just in time. I've made a fresh pot."

"You all right?" Lucas asked, concern limned on his face.

"Yeah. No. I don't know." She flopped into a chair next to them and flipped through the papers.

All of them had stories of the "Highgate Vampire" and included several CCTV images. None showed her clearly, but there were a couple in which Montague could be seen clearly, and Lucas and Richard were somewhat recognizable.

"This is bad," Della said. "Really bad."

Montague set a cup of tea in front of her as if it might solve everything.

"Don't bother reading the articles," Montague said. "Just a load of rubbish."

Della turned to Lucas. "You never told me he was supposed to be a vampire."

"A modern invention. I didn't tell you because I wanted you to take all of this seriously."

"After what I've been through, how could I take it any other way?"

"Glad to hear it. Oh, Richard called. He went to the NHS and got a pass for the rest of the week. He's retrieved your things and is reading that book you bought. He'll be down tonight. He has some things to do before he leaves Oxford, though, and won't arrive until quite late."

"How did he fool the doctor?"

"I don't know. I'm sure he has his ways. It's a pity we can't have him with us tonight."

Despair tugged at Della. She had an overwhelming urge to leap out of her seat and run back up to her bedroom. They were planning something, and she was supposed to be a part of it.

Somehow she summoned the strength to remain in her seat and ask, "What do we have to do?"

"We have to face dear old Ebenezer."

Della cringed. "We can't get back in the cemetery. There must be police patrolling there."

"No, we don't have to go there," Lucas said and then smiled. "In fact, I'm going to take you out for a pub dinner."

"Come again?"

"It's an old pub that Ebenezer haunted." When Lucas saw Della's reaction, he quickly added, "Sorry. Poor choice of words."

"What's the point of going there?"

"We're hoping you or I, more likely you, will pick up some vibrations from the spirit. It's not on a ley line, so we should be fairly safe."

"Fairly safe," Della grumbled. "Meaning fairly unsafe."

"Drink one for me," Montague said and gestured at the newspapers spread out on the table. "I shan't be leaving the house for quite some time."

They got ready to leave. At the door, Montague gave Della a little bone amulet suspended on a leather strap. Viking runes were engraved on it, and the strap was knotted in three places with complex knots.

"This should afford you some protection. Best of luck."

Normally she would have laughed the amulet off as worthless junk. Now she simply nodded, put it around her neck, and hid it under her scarf and shirt.

The pub was in north Islington, about twenty minutes away by bus, and down a little side street. It looked like the oldest building in the area. Della's practiced eye picked out many postwar constructions of steel and concrete and others belonging to the Victorian era of ostentatious brickwork, but the little two-story building at the end of the dead-end lane was of timber frame construction with an aged, swaybacked roof whose slate tiles were covered in moss. The windows were small and paned with thick glass distorted by ripples, indicating they had been made at an early date, before blowing large window panes became feasible. The faded wooden sign outside announced the pub to be John Dee's Cave.

"This building looks Tudor or Elizabethan," Della said.

Lucas nodded. "A rare survival. This was all fields back then, and the city grew around the pub. It is perhaps the oldest in London. John Dee was court magician to Queen Elizabeth I."

"I've heard of him. Wasn't he a fraud?"

Lucas chuckled. "Perhaps. He certainly was controversial. But we're not here for him so much as for good old Ebenezer. He often held meetings here because of the association with Dr. Dee. The earlier mage supposedly did rituals in a cave beneath the pub."

"You don't sound terribly convinced."

"An important thing to remember when dealing with the magical world is to keep an open mind. An equally important thing to remember is not to believe everything you hear."

The pub's interior was dim, with exposed wooden beams and various small tables scattered here and there. A fat old man leaned against the bar, talking loudly to a bored barman about football while sipping a pint. Only a few of the other tables were taken—a scattering of solitary drinkers, a middle-aged couple who were kissing more than they were drinking, and three skinny girls dressed all in black who barely looked old enough to be in there. They had about a dozen facial piercings among them. One was laying out a deck of tarot cards, the colorful images making a pattern across the scarred old tabletop.

"Why don't you sit over there while I get a couple of pints and a menu," Lucas said, indicating a corner table. It was the table next to the three Goth girls, but she supposed he wanted to sit there because of the hole in the floor that was covered with Plexiglass.

Della went over to it and saw it was a vertical shaft going down about five feet before opening to a small chamber in the stone. A brass ring around the opening to the hole said in cursive script, John Dee's Fabled Cave.

Leaning down to get a better look, she saw the walls had been crudely hacked out of the limestone. She could still see the original marks left by the pick. It wasn't a cave at all.

One of the Goth girls muttered something about tourists. Della tensed and sat down.

You're fighting spirits, and you're worried about what a few poseurs think?

Sad to say, she did. The tables were close to one another, and there were plenty of free tables farther away. Della was crowding them, and the looks they shot her made her know it.

She fidgeted until Lucas returned with the drinks. The Goth girls gave him appreciative looks, which made Della smile.

Sorry, girls, he's with me.

Cassandra's warning came back to her.

He was hurt badly at a young age. That's made him selfish. Be careful, Della. You won't be able to change him.

"Sorry for dragging you to this rather dreary

place for dinner," Lucas said, handing her the menu. "It seems we're always spending time in places more suited to me than to you."

"It's all right," Della replied.

"Could use a bit of a dusting," he said, looking around. "And don't go to the toilets if you know what's good for you. But the food's actually edible, unlike most pubs. They cook it rather than reheat prepackaged meals."

Della studied the menu. The bartender extricated himself from his football conversation with the aging drunk and came over. Lucas ordered a gammon steak and Della a fish and chips.

"I'll keep this for a minute," Della said when he reached for the menu. "I wanted to read the history on the back."

A loud scoff came from the other table. Della tried to ignore it.

Straight-A student, and you still get nervous raising your hand in class. Champion fencer, and you still feel more comfortable when your mask is on. Fighting the paranormal, and you care about the opinions of somebody who thinks tarot cards are a way to see the future.

How did you get like this?

That had always been a mystery to her. She had

nothing in her past that could have broken her spirit so. No perverted uncles or overbearing mothers. No siblings dying of cancer. No disfiguring illnesses. Nothing. Sure, she had endured a fair degree of bullying at school, but that occurred *because* she was shy. It didn't cause it.

Her life had simply always been this way.

She thought she was getting better now that she was totally in her comfort zone in graduate school, as much as anything could ever be in her comfort zone. But now she had lost her advisor and her boyfriend, and with the hidden world intruding in on the familiar one, she was in danger of losing her sanity.

Get back to work.

She started reading the history on the back of the menu.

"Welcome to John Dee's Cave, London's oldest surviving pub, serving customers with fine food and drink since 1498. Originally called Merlin's Cave, it was built atop an ancient cave used for Druidical rites since prehistoric times. The wizard Merlin is said to have performed magic here."

Said by whom? Della wondered. *The pub landlord?*

"The pub has always been a meeting ground for mystics, spiritual seekers, and those who dabble in the magical arts. The famous occultist John Dee (1527-1609), astrologer to Queen Elizabeth I, often met here with fellow occultists such as Edward Kelley. He used the premises for the performance of magical rituals to predict the future and commune with angels. Since such practices were illegal at the time, they would perform them in the cave beneath the pub. Access was through a secret passage in a hidden panel in the wall, which has been sealed off for many years. You can still see the cave where Merlin and John Dee practiced magic through a hole in the pub floor.

"John Dee's Cave welcomes practitioners of all faiths from near and far and hosts many regular meetings of London's occult societies."

She put the menu down and looked at Lucas.

"Is any of this true?"

Lucas shrugged and smiled. "Are the histories on pub menus ever true?"

Della shrugged. "I'm having trouble knowing what is true and what isn't at the moment."

"Indeed. Well, that cave beneath our feet is most likely an old wine cellar. It certainly isn't a natural cave. This really has been a meeting place for occult circles for many years, though. Our man Ebenezer used to meet here with his louche friends. Are you picking anything up?"

Della sat quietly for a moment. "No. I'm not feeling a thing."

Lucas nodded slightly in the direction of the other table.

"Picking anything up from them?" he whispered.

"Hostility and superficiality."

"See? You are a sensitive."

Della chuckled. "I'm glad you don't take this entirely seriously."

"You'll keep a firmer hold on your sanity if you don't."

"Is this on a ley line? I'm not getting that funny feeling I got at the other places of power."

Della couldn't believe a sentence like that had just come out of her mouth. Life was really taking some strange turns.

"No, it's not. And the 'cave' beneath our feet has no distinct power either. There is some residual power from all the rituals done in it, of course, but you haven't had any training, and thus, you probably can't feel that. I can't feel much myself. It isn't helped by all the charlatans who come here and perform rituals that produce absolutely nothing.

This community is filled with people who will believe anything."

Della glanced at the trio at the next table, who had stopped sneering and were absorbed in the layout of tarot cards.

"Like tarot cards and vampires?"

"Precisely. Oh, the tarot can be useful for divination, but all it does is channel the individual's own Talent." Lucas lowered his voice when he said, "Or lack thereof. You're right to hold tarot cards in low esteem—and vampires."

"Oh, I think vampires are fascinating."

He cocked his head. "Really?"

Della laughed. "I read far too many fantasy books growing up. It gets in your blood."

"And look where that's led you."

"Yeah, really. As I got older, I wanted to study the real thing."

Now Lucas looked truly surprised. "The real thing?"

"Not the way *you* mean it. I mean studying the folklore and legends that gave rise to these beliefs. Have you ever read *Vampires, Burial & Death* by Paul Barber?"

"My aunt has given me an extensive reading list, but I can't say that is on it."

"It's fascinating and purely scientific. Barber looked at the original court transcripts and early investigations of vampire reports from the sixteenth to the eighteenth centuries. He found they followed a pattern. Someone would die in a village, and they'd be buried. Soon after, someone else would die. If the first person had been a bit strange, perhaps an outsider or a local troublemaker estranged from the church, they'd be suspected of the second death. The body would be dug up and would be found to be swollen, with a florid face and blood around the lips. The eyes and mouth might be open. Often the body would have moved in the coffin."

"Really? That's rather macabre."

"Yes and no. You see, Professor Barber consulted with morticians and criminal forensics experts and found out that all those things could be explained by postmortem changes in the body. The bloating comes from the accumulation of gases in the stomach and lungs as the flesh decomposes. This pushes blood up the windpipe to come out the mouth. The pressure can also open the eyes. Sometimes blood even comes out of there too. Now, early people would bury a body quickly, before it stank, so they wouldn't know about any of these natural processes. When they saw a body of the suspect like this, they'd feel sure they'd found a vampire and put a stake through its heart. That explains why so many reports talk about the vampire screaming when it was staked. The gasses would come shooting out like a popped balloon. Sometimes it would even spew out blood onto the vampire hunters."

"You're actually grinning. And here I thought you were such a nice girl. But it doesn't explain why a vampire would move in its coffin. What about rigor mortis?"

Della was vaguely aware of the Goth girls listening in. They weren't scoffing now.

"That's only temporary. It goes away after a few days. Most people don't know that in the modern world, and with villagers burying the dead within a day or two after they'd passed on, they certainly wouldn't know that. With all the gasses expanding in the body, the body can shift and sometimes even end up on its side."

"Interesting. But that still doesn't explain the later deaths or the sightings of the dead person moving around the cemetery."

Della raised her hand and gave him a smug smile. "The later deaths could be because the flu was passing through the village or simply pure chance.

As for the sightings, superstitious people will make up all sorts of things in their heads."

The Goth girls muttered something and went back to their tarot cards. Lucas leaned in close.

"Don't start backtracking. While there is plenty of nonsense in the occult world, you know as well as I do there are true things too."

Della bit her lip and nodded.

Their food came, and they ate in companionable silence, each trying to pick up signals from the hidden world. It occurred to her that to the rest of the pub, this looked as much like a "date table," as a waitress friend of hers always used to say, as the table with the kissing couple.

The reality was quite different, or was it? She couldn't deny she had feelings for Lucas, and yet she couldn't really sort them out. They had been through so much danger together. They had even saved each other's lives. That was bound to create a bond. But she could say the same about Richard, and her feelings toward him were different. Richard was becoming a close friend. Lucas didn't quite fit into that category.

He certainly was attractive and kind. It confused her that he had never made a move. Did he not have any feelings for her like that? Did she even want him to have those feelings?

Sad to say, he had a number of strikes against him. Lots of emotional baggage, for one, although she shouldn't be judging people on *that* basis. And the occultism stuff had always turned her off. Now that she was beginning to believe in some of it, it turned her off even more. Her few boyfriends had always been refuges from the stress of the world. Someone deep into the occult was the exact opposite of what she needed right now.

It wasn't so much that he believed in it but the company it made him keep. She had always felt that you could judge someone by their friends, and other than Richard, in that category, he came up short. Autumn was vain and self-absorbed. Cassandra had been downright catty. Della shouldn't have to save someone's life in order to get courtesy out of them.

A friend, she told herself. *Keep him as a friend. He probably isn't interested anyway.*

That conclusion made her sadder than she anticipated.

To distract herself, she focused her perception on her surroundings, trying to pick up any of the inexplicable sensations she had felt in the other locations.

Nothing. Not even a whisper. If Ebenezer King

had ever performed any black magic here, the residual energy from that had been erased by generations of silly amateurs like the three at the next table.

Their dinner finished, Lucas insisted on paying. "A weak form of apology for getting you into this mess."

Della didn't argue. She deserved a lot more than a dinner.

"I didn't sense anything," Della said.

"No, neither did I. We can't come up with a success every time, I suppose."

They stood.

"Yeah, no power here at all," Della said in a slightly louder voice. "This isn't a place for occultists, just tourists."

The Goth girls glared at her. She turned her back so they wouldn't see her blush and headed for the door.

I can't believe I just did that. That's not like me at all.

They stepped out into the night. It had turned unseasonably cool. Della almost asked for Lucas's sweater until she remembered it had been Cassandra's keepsake for several years. The woman had probably slept with it. Despite the bad things Cassandra had said about him, it was obvious she still had feelings for the guy. Did she want to get him back? Was that why she had given Della that lecture? To get rid of the competition?

They walked down the little dead-end lane, now dark and quiet in the summer night. As they approached where it intersected with a bigger street, Della noticed a van with the logo of a plumbing company parked to one side.

She stopped dead. It was the same van the kidnappers had used to snatch Autumn.

The back door opened, and the same two burly men jumped out and ran for them.

16

LUCAS SPOTTED the van the instant Della stopped and let out a gasp. He squared up. This time he was ready for them. He had helped out his uncle Philip for years on the sheep farm and had plenty of muscle. He was also a good deal younger than these two bruisers.

There was only one problem—he wasn't an experienced fighter, and they were.

He swung at the first man, but the guy ducked, and Lucas connected with nothing but air. Then the man planted a fist in Lucas's ribs. He hissed with pain, backpedaled, then gave the plumber a good right cross as he moved to follow. That stopped the plumber in his tracks. Lucas wound up for another punch that would have laid him low but got stopped mid-swing by a sudden pain and a blinding flash of light.

The other plumber had dived into the fight and slugged him a good one on the side of the head.

Lucas staggered to the side, not stopping until his shoulder banged against the wall of a nearby building. He shook his head to clear it and saw Della struggling with one of the plumbers, smacking him hard against the face. He grunted in resentment and pain, squeezing her around the middle and hauling her toward the van.

A man stuck his head out of the driver's-side window.

"Get a move on, will you?"

The man who had hit Lucas glanced back at the sound of the voice. Lucas took his moment of distraction to rush him.

He had intended on knocking him off his feet and going to help Della. He was only half successful. Ramming into the man gave him a good opportunity to punch Lucas, and they both ended up going down.

Lucas got up first. After scrambling to his feet and taking a moment to steady himself, he rushed over to the van just as Della got tossed inside. He struck out at her captor, giving him a glancing blow to the face before getting a much harder one to his own.

Then the opponent he had bowled over smacked him in the back of the neck.

Lucas fell like a sack of oats. Dimly he felt rough hands pull him up. He tried to fight back but couldn't get his arms and legs to work. They tossed him into the back of the van.

The door slammed, and they were plunged into darkness. Della banged on the back of the door. Lucas could hear her shake the handle.

"It's locked from outside!" she cried.

Lucas sat up, his entire body in pain. Suddenly a light stabbed his eyes. A small slit had opened in the wall between the cab of the van and the back. He saw the shadow of a hand flicker across the light and heard a metallic clink on the floor, and the slit slammed shut.

A soft hiss came from the floor. A sweet, pungent odor filled his nostrils.

"They're gassing us!" Della shouted.

He clamped the neckline of his sweater over his face and tried to hold his breath.

Too late. His head swam. He exhaled, trying to get all the gas out of his lungs. In the darkness next to him, he heard Della choking.

Lucas's lungs began to burn, desperate for more air. He got on his back, steadied himself as his head spun from the movement, and kicked out at the door with both feet.

The clang of his shoes hitting metal sounded distant, weak. He didn't know whether that was the drug or because he simply couldn't kick with any force. He kicked again. It sounded even weaker.

Then his lungs rebelled, and he took a deep breath of air.

The cloth he had bunched up against his nose did not save him. His body succumbed to a wave of disorientation. He tried to kick out again, but only one leg obeyed his orders, to thud uselessly against the hard steel.

And after, that he could move no more.

For the rest of that long ride, Lucas did not lose consciousness. Neither did Della, whom he could hear whimpering beside him. Neither had the strength to move or even speak to one another. They were entombed in their own weakness, unable to act but able to feel and hear and think.

Think about what was in store for them at the end of that drive.

Lucas fought off panic and tried to focus. He had heard of a method, something Aunt Mary had mentioned but not really demonstrated, a type of mental communication between practitioners who shared blood and a mental bond.

Aunt Mary was the only one in his life who fit the bill.

"I don't want you in my head all the time!" Lucas had joked when she had offered to teach him.

Aunt Mary had told him that it didn't work like that, but still he had resisted learning it. Having such an ability would be like having a mobile phone inside your skull twenty-four hours a day.

Now he wished he had asked for a few lessons.

What had she said? Something about mental focus. Had there been a ritual attached? Some preparation the two people had to do first before the communication could work? It had been one of those eager lectures over dinner that he had tuned out of. Why hadn't he paid more attention to his magical studies? Aunt Mary and Richard were always pestering him to study more, and he'd only done the bare minimum to keep them quiet.

He let out a long, slow breath, willing himself to relax. He tried to clear his mind, pushing down the panic and setting aside the grisly thoughts of what would happen when the van finally stopped.

The farm. He pictured the farm. The ancient

oak at the boundary stone, that stone that formed a power point along a ley line and had been set there centuries ago, maybe even as far back as the now-vanished stone circle atop which the Anglo-Saxon church had been built. He pictured himself walking up the path to the house then passing through the front door and down the hall to the kitchen. He pictured the warmth and the cooking smells.

No, the library. It was too late in the evening for her to be in the kitchen. She was probably reading in the library.

Did it matter whether he picked the right room or not? He let that thought slide away. He shouldn't get distracted. Perhaps if he pictured her in the library, that would secure the connection no matter where she was. Or not. He had no bloody idea.

Don't think about that! Focus!

The library. He pictured the old armchair where she liked to sit. The faded green fabric worn smooth on the arms from years of use. The wonky leg he had promised to mend but hadn't gotten around to because Aunt Mary wouldn't give up her favorite seat for the day or so the job would take.

And then he wasn't imagining it anymore. He was seeing it. Images of her came in brief flashes as one gets with fragmentary dreams on the border between wakefulness and sleep.

She was there, sitting in the seat just like he thought.

His excitement broke the connection. He forced himself to calm down and repeat the process. Slowly, the images returned. Steadied.

Aunt Mary closed the book in her lap and looked right at him.

I need help. I've been taken by the same people who took Autumn. I'm somewhere in central London in the back of a white plumbers' van. There's a company name on the side. It's ...

The van jerked to a stop. The thin thread of connection Lucas felt with his aunt snapped. The back door of the van opened, and the interior was flooded with light.

Lucas opened his eyes and blinked. The van was parked inside a concrete garage. Lucas smelled oil and damp. Two of his captors stood there, watching him.

He had failed.

They dragged him out by the legs.

"Mind his head. The boss wants him in one piece."

They set him on the floor. The concrete felt cold.

"What about this piece?" the other plumber said, jabbing his finger in Della's direction and grinning.

"Later. Boss wants to see them both. We'll get our chance."

"I want the toff, but I'll settle for this one."

A third man appeared. Lucas recognized him as the driver. Two picked up Della and carried her out of view. Lucas was so weakened by the gas that he couldn't even turn his head to see what they were doing with her. The driver rummaged through his pockets and removed his keys, wallet, and phone. Then he put his arms under Lucas's shoulders and dragged him through a doorway, his shoes scraping along the concrete.

His captor pulled him down a long, carpeted hallway with wood-paneled walls. Dark oil paintings and the heads of deer and wild boar adorned them. The place exuded old money. They passed several doors, all of which were closed.

They stopped. Lucas heard the rattle of a key and a door opening, and the man holding him dragged him into a room.

"Lucas!" a voice cried.

It was Autumn. Lucas tried to call back but only managed an incoherent mumble.

"Lucas, answer me! What have you done to

them?" He heard the rattle of metal on metal. Lucas was laid down on a carpet. Still unable to move his head, all he could see was a ceiling with a light installed in an old-fashioned crystal fixture. The driver moved out of view, and the door closed. The key rattled again, and Lucas knew they had been locked inside.

"Oh, Lucas, I can't believe they got you and your friend too. Why can't you speak? Oh my god, they've drugged you or something! I can't help you. I'm handcuffed to this bed. I haven't left this room since I was kidnapped, except once when they posed that photo. You must have gotten my signal. I didn't dare do anything else. They said they'd kill me on the spot if I did. I should have let them." Autumn sobbed. "They've been... bleeding me."

Lucas went cold, a sick feeling settling in the pit of his stomach. So Montague's guess had been right. They were using her for a royal blood ritual.

Montague had mentioned something else too.

The most powerful blood rituals ended in sacrifice.

17

EVEN WITHOUT THE GAS, Della felt sure she wouldn't have been able to move. She had become paralyzed with fear. These monsters were bleeding Autumn dry and had joked about what they wanted to do to her and Della. Actually laughed about it. They were capable of anything, and she knew in her heart that she was going to experience the worst sort of torture before she died.

That was why, when the door opened after a few minutes, Della's heart nearly seized up. She jerked, cried out, and realized she could move.

Although not much. She flopped around like a fish thrown on the beach. She could hear Lucas trying to move beside her on the floor.

She raised her head and saw a man standing at

the doorway. He wasn't one of the thugs from the van. He looked more refined.

And far more frightening.

He stood a little over six feet tall and was trim and muscular and of an indeterminate age. Not young but healthy enough not to look too old. His head was shaved, and Della could tell that he had gone bald up top. His eyes were brown and had a dead quality about them. When they fixed on Della, they did not seem to see her as a human being but more as an unwanted object.

Nothing about his appearance made Della recoil in fear. It was more his manner, or perhaps the better word was *aura*. It was not a word Della was accustomed to using, but how else to describe the sensation of menace and evil that she felt at a gut level when she looked at him?

Della tried to crawl away. Her limbs were still clumsy, and she could barely back off a few inches across the floor.

"The gas should be wearing off now," he said in a refined public-school accent that spoke of a lifetime of wealth and privilege. "You, Lucas Lancaster, can you speak?"

"H-How do you know my name?" Lucas's words came out slurred.

"Ah, good, so you can speak. As for your name, we've been watching Autumn for some time, so we have come to know of her associates. Especially those who delve into the hidden arts."

Montague, Della thought. *He's in danger too.*

He turned to study Della. "You are new to me. An innocent tourist caught up in something she doesn't understand? Or perhaps more."

He knelt beside her and placed a hand on her forehead. Della yanked her head away, but he grabbed her jaw with the other hand to hold her steady and put his hand on her forehead again. He closed his eyes. Della felt a tingling go through her head and shuddered.

After a moment, he opened his eyes and smiled.

"Oh my, something much more than a tourist. But new to this situation, oh yes. You have made a poor choice of friends, whatever your name is."

He stood. "Perhaps you'll prove useful before I dispose of you. Autumn here has proven vital to our operations. Are you an occultist Mr. Lancaster brought in to help?"

"N-No," Della replied, trying to get her mouth to form words. "I'm just a friend. I-I don't know anything about this. The other night was the first time I even met Autumn."

"You had never met Autumn before? That, I believe, because I would have noticed someone with so much Talent. But just a friend who knows nothing?" The man clucked his tongue and shook his head. "Oh no, you most certainly pose a danger to us. I would not be surprised if you were the one who dispelled our water weird."

Della didn't reply. The man turned to Lucas and gave him a nudge in the ribs with the toe of his boot. Not a kick, more the threat of one, and a not-too-subtle humiliation.

"Who else do you have on your team? I detected three more. One will join you shortly. The other two have eluded me."

"We've informed the police," Lucas said. "They're looking for you. If you let us go, you might have enough lead time to escape."

Their captor smiled. "Silly boy. Of course you haven't informed the police. What would you tell them? That you're the chap in all the newspapers? That you've uncovered a royal blood ritual? Come now. Tell me of the two others."

"Go to hell."

The man nodded in Della's direction. "My assistants want this one. Shall I let them go to it?"

Lucas paled. Della felt like throwing up.

The man smiled again. His smiles were the most frightening thing about him.

"Think upon it. They're out collecting Mr. James as we speak. I wish I could have gone along with them, because there is so much of his stock I'd like to appropriate, but I am a bit busy at the moment. Speaking of…"

He pulled a hypodermic from his pocket and strolled over to Autumn.

Della was able to turn her head now and watched with horror as the occultist held down a whimpering Autumn and jabbed her arm with the hypo. He pulled back the plunger, and the tube filled with deep-red liquid. Then he yanked out the needle and pressed a cotton swab against the hole.

"Hold it there," he ordered his victim.

Della noticed the sheets were spotted with blood.

He strolled to the door and turned.

"I'll need your answer when they come back, Mr. Lancaster, or I'll give my assistants a bonus in the form of your American friend."

With that, he closed and locked the door.

For several minutes, no one spoke. Della was stunned with disgust, Lucas looked ashamed, and Autumn sobbed quietly.

At last, Della struggled to her feet. With uncertain steps, she went to the door and listened. Silence. She surveyed the room. Other than the bed, there were no furnishings. There were no windows and nothing on the walls except a few rectangles of darker paint where pictures had once hung. The nails had been removed. She didn't see any cameras or obvious listening devices.

Lucas got to his feet and stumbled over to Autumn.

"Have they told you anything about the ritual?" he asked as he tested the handcuffs. They were locked to the heavy steel bedframe.

"Nothing."

"Have they performed any rituals in here? Have you seen anyone else?"

Autumn shook her head.

Della went over to the bed and examined it. The legs were attached to the frame by screws.

"If we could unscrew these legs, we could have some nice clubs," Della said.

"Unscrew them with what?" Lucas asked.

"Let's try our belt buckles."

They did, but they were too thick to get into the slit of the screw. Then Della noticed Autumn wore earrings that were little gold disks, like a pair of suns.

"Give me one of your earrings," Della said.

"But they're gold," Autumn said. "They're way too soft."

"Let's try."

Autumn nodded. Della took an earring and inserted it into the screw. With a bit of effort, it turned. The earring bent slightly and slipped out of the slot. Della saw she had scraped off a thin veneer of gold to reveal steel underneath.

Solid gold, eh?

Turning the earring in her hand, she used an unbent portion to turn the screw until it was almost out of the hole, then she started working on the second screw on the leg.

"Why don't you unscrew me?" Autumn begged.

"This won't work on the handcuffs, and you're secured to the headboard. I could remove that, but you'd end up having to carry it around with you. First let's get ourselves some weapons. Those goons will be back soon, and we need to get ready. If we can overpower them, we can get the keys and free you."

That seemed like a long shot. At least it was better than waiting around to be abused by those creeps.

The second screw was rusty and a lot more stubborn. Della cursed as she scraped her already-tender fingers trying to turn it. Lucas got Autumn's other earring and got to work on a second leg of the bed.

"I'm surprised they're not guarding us better," Lucas said.

"This looks like a converted guest bedroom," Della replied. "I don't think this guy thought he'd have so many prisoners. He only had one set of hand-cuffs, for example."

"Perhaps you're right, but that door looks stout enough."

Della nodded. It was a thick, old-style oaken door. Smashing it would take a lot of strength and would make way too much noise.

After a few minutes, and having thoroughly ruined Autumn's fake gold earrings, they got the screws loose on two legs of the bed.

"Now all we need to do is lift the bed, and these legs should pop right off," Lucas said, wiping his brow.

Della nodded. "Let's try to do this quietly. That guy might be close by."

"I can't get off the bed," Autumn said.

Lucas gave her an encouraging smile. "It's all right. I'll lift you and the bed. It will be like tossing a sheep into the sheep dip. Della, when I lift it, pull those legs off."

Lucas planted his feet, bent at the knees, and grabbed the frame of the bed. With a grunt, he straightened his legs, and the end of the bed rose a foot. Della yanked one of the legs off, gritting her teeth when it came off easier than she expected and *thunk*ed against the floor. She hurried to the next one and pulled that off. Lucas gently set the end of the bed down. Autumn was still stuck on the bed, which now lay at an angle.

Della and Lucas hefted the metal legs. They were steel tubes, light and hard and about as long as a policeman's nightstick. The perfect weapon.

They positioned themselves on either side of the door.

"Let's try not to get in each other's way," Della said. "When they open up, let me swing first."

"I'm stronger," Lucas said.

"I'm angrier."

"But—"

Della glared at him. "They weren't looking at you like a piece of meat."

"I wish I could hit them with one of those," Autumn said. "Those beasts have been saying crude things to me ever since I got here. Their boss won't let them touch me, though. That's to make me cooperate."

They stood there for a minute, tense and poised, their clubs raised above their heads and ready to swing. Della felt her heart racing. Could she really smack someone upside the head with a length of steel?

Yes, in this situation, she could. She thought.

She wouldn't know until the moment came.

Minutes passed. Their arms grew tired, and they lowered the pipes. Della remained tense, ready to raise it again the instant the door opened.

"Okay, so we hit these guys and bust out of here," Della said. "Then what?"

Lucas shrugged. "I have no idea. Find the keys and then call the police, I suppose."

"What if they have guns?"

"This is England."

"They're using your friend for blood sacrifices."

"Well, if they do have guns, we're all dead, so how about we not talk about it, all right?"

Della shrugged. That was a bit testy.

"Upstairs!" Autumn said.

"What?" Della asked, not taking her eyes off the door.

"Once when they... bled me, the bald man told

his assistant to take the hypodermic upstairs. I think that's where they're doing the rituals."

Della nodded. Maybe Autumn wasn't so useless after all.

Don't get cocky, she chided herself. *You could end up equally useless in this fight.*

She didn't have long to find out. A minute later, she heard the key rattle in the lock.

18

THEIR CAPTORS WEREN'T SO incautious as to walk into the room without checking on them first. The door opened a crack, and the van driver's suspicious face appeared. His eyes widened, and he slammed the door shut.

Or at least tried to. Lucas kicked it open. The door smacked into the driver, and he stumbled back with a curse.

All three of the men from the van stood in the hallway, two of them holding Montague between them. He looked as drugged as they had been. Lucas raised his pipe to swing.

And got shoved aside by Della, who swung at the driver. The man brought up his arm to protect his head, and the steel club connected with a sickening crack of bone.

The man ran off, cradling his arm and screaming. Della stepped into the hallway and raised her club again.

One of their other captors let go of Montague and grabbed Della's pipe. They struggled for a second, turning in a way that kept Lucas from getting a good hit on him. The other man grabbed at Della, and Lucas jabbed him in the temple with his pipe. The plumber stumbled back with a grunt just as the man wrestling with Della tore the pipe out of her grasp.

Della was smart enough to dive to the side, and Lucas clocked the man a good one before he got a chance to use his newly acquired weapon.

That one went down, but the plumber Lucas had jabbed with the bed post tackled him, pinning his arms to his sides. Lucas struggled, wrenching his body to try to break free, and they ended up on the floor with the plumber on top.

The chap was the typical working-class bruiser with impressive muscles and an equally impressive paunch thanks to a steady diet of lager and kebab. Lucas struggled to breathe as he got pressed under the man's weight.

Whatever his eating habits, the man knew how to fight. He shifted his body to get one of Lucas's arms pinned then pinned the other one with his forearm and used his free hand to smack Lucas in the face.

While he couldn't get much leverage, it hurt quite enough, and there were more coming.

Lucas suffered two more punches before he heard a thud. The man jerked and then fell unconscious over him.

"Ugh," Lucas grunted, pushing the man off. "That was unpleasant. Oh dear, my nose has turned into a geyser of blood again."

"You're welcome," Della said. She stood over him with the pipe in her hand.

"Thank you," Lucas said, picking himself up.

Two of the plumbers were out cold on the floor. Montague lay nearby, a helpless victim of the gas. The third plumber had run off. They could hear him screaming somewhere in the house.

Lucas checked the two men's pockets. No keys.

"Bloody hell. The one that's scarpered must have them."

"We have to go after him," Della said.

"Don't leave me!"

Autumn's cry from the bedroom made them hesitate. She lay on the blood-speckled bed, still hand-cuffed, stuck at an angle because they had removed the legs.

Della came to a decision first.

"We have to leave if we want to free you. We'll come back. I promise."

Della ran down the hall. Lucas gave a final look at his two friends and followed.

The hallway led past several closed doors they didn't bother to check and then up a flight of stairs. They ended up in another hallway with a window and realized that they had been in a cellar and were now on the ground floor. Another set of staircases continued up. A light shone in the hall and on the stairwell, but the two rooms they could see on this level were dark.

Voices from above made them move up the stairs. Lucas briefly wondered if it would be better to smash through a window and make their escape, going to the police and bringing reinforcements, but Della could not be stopped.

It was probably the right decision. Leaving Autumn and Montague alone with these people for even a couple of minutes might prove fatal.

Rushing headlong into the unknown might be

fatal too. Lucas grabbed Della, stopped her enraged rush upstairs, and got in front of her. That threat to her virtue had really gotten her mad. They heard footsteps from above. More voices. Lucas spread out a cautionary hand, and Della nodded, realizing now that silence would be their best ally.

They moved as quietly as they could up the stairs, their steel clubs at the ready.

"Hurry up and get it!" they heard the bald man shout. "Get it all. There isn't much time."

At the top of the stairs, they came to a hall with a few closed doors. An open doorway led to a study lined with bookshelves. The windows looked out on a dark garden and an empty street some distance away, looking forlorn under the yellow streetlamps.

They entered the room, looking around for their things but not finding them.

Lucas hesitated, tempted once again to break a window and scream for help.

But that would give away their position, and surprising their enemies was their best hope for survival.

In the end, it was their enemies who surprised them. Suddenly the lights went out.

Lucas froze. In the dim light filtering in through

the window, he saw Della's eyes go wide. He tiptoed to the doorway and peered down the stairs. No light came from below. He heard a distant cry. Autumn. Calling for help. She must be terrified to suddenly be stuck in the darkness, still handcuffed to the bed with only the helpless Montague as company.

He fumbled for the light switch and found it next to the door. He flicked it on and off several times. Nothing. They must have cut the mains.

Lucas cocked an ear. Silence. The others had to be up here. There didn't seem to be another story to this house. But they were keeping quiet.

Waiting.

Della looked at him, an unspoken question on her face. Lucas shrugged. They could barely see each other in this room. If they moved away from it, they would be all but blind, groping around an unfamiliar house that their enemies were intimately familiar with.

At the top of the stairs was another window, shrouded with curtains. Lucas crept over and opened them. That gave them a bit more light. They could see another distant streetlamp and the dark bulk of a neighboring house cut off by a tall fence and nothing more. If they screamed, most likely no one would hear them. Whatever they had to face, they would have to face it alone.

An anguished gasp came from down the hallway. The driver who had gotten his arm broken? He was behind one of those doors, hiding but no doubt armed as well. And what about his nameless boss?

A glimmer of light caught his eye, coming from the crack beneath the door at the very end of the hall. The light was wavering and yellow, so he guessed it was a candle.

A candle. A ritual.

A low intonation in Latin told him he was correct.

Lucas gestured with his club in the direction of the door. Della nodded.

She leaned in close and whispered, "What kind of spell is that?"

Her hot breath on his ear gave him lovely sensations that he didn't have time to enjoy.

"I don't know," he whispered back.

Her frustrated look was obvious even in the poor light.

"You're the wizard."

"I am anything but a wizard."

My Latin isn't even good enough to know what he's saying.

Della shook her head and listened for a moment.

"It's Latin," she whispered in his ear again, giving him a delicious feeling entirely inappropriate for the circumstances. "But it's medieval Latin, and I can't quite get it. Something about 'the signs of night and water.'"

Lucas's heart skipped a beat. He had read that phrase before in one of Aunt Mary's books. It was a summoning of the dead. Water was a life essence and also had aspects of motion, and night was the abode of those who had passed on. Combining the two gave the dead new life.

Ebenezer King. He's summoning Ebenezer King.

"We have to get in there now!" he said. "Stop him before he completes the ritual."

They rushed down the hallway, guided by the light. When they got halfway there, a side door flew open, and a dark figure leapt out, wielding a machete. The faint light from the window gleamed off sharp steel.

Luckily Lucas's attacker was fighting half blind. Otherwise, he would have taken his head off with the first swing. Instead Lucas jerked back, bumping into Della, the machete whooshing an inch from his face.

Lucas swung with his metal club, but the man

parried then brought up his machete for another swing.

Lucas and Della backpedaled. This wasn't the big bruiser whose arm had been broken or the bald man in charge. This was somebody new. Lean. Small. Aggressive.

The man made another swing, trying to gut him. Lucas jumped back again, and the machete slashed a deep scrape in the wood paneling.

Now it was Lucas's turn. He swung the metal pipe, missed, then made a backswing before his opponent had a chance to strike again.

The man parried but must have had a weak grip because the machete flew out of his hand.

Before Lucas could knock him out, the fellow yelped and ducked back into the darkened room, disappearing into the shadows.

Lucas hesitated. The chanting continued. He didn't want to give this man his back, but the greater danger lay ahead.

Della decided for him. Picking up the machete with her free hand, she strode to the doorway. Lucas followed and tried the knob. Locked.

He backed up, tensed his shoulder, and rushed at the door. The stout oak shook in the frame but held. Della took a position a little way off, watching the doorway through which the machete man had fled. No sound came from that direction. Whatever that man was doing, he was being quiet about it. That got Lucas worried.

Lucas hit the door again, hissing as his shoulder flared with pain. Bucking up, he rammed it again with his other shoulder. This time he was rewarded with a cracking sound.

"One more, and I'll get it," Lucas said.

Something made him pause. He glanced behind him. No, nothing there.

Then he realized what it was.

The chanting had stopped.

His skin prickled. The temperature in the hallway began to drop. Lucas backed away from the door.

"We're too late. Let's get back to the others and get the hell out of here."

A faint, luminous white mist issued from beneath the door. Della yelped. They both hurried down the hallway.

Only to get tackled by the man hiding in the side room.

He managed to take out both of them at the same time, leaping from the shadows with his arms wide.

They hit the far wall together and fell in a heap onto the floor.

Lucas dropped his pipe. Struggling to untangle himself from Della, he got smacked on the chin by a fist. He lashed out, making a good connection. The machete man grunted and rolled away.

Giving a clear view of what was forming at the end of the hallway.

19

THE MIST at the end of the hallway began to coalesce into two shapes, one larger than the other. Della's heart beat wildly as she sat up, moving back away from the apparition. The man who attacked them cackled, sprang away from the tangle they had all been in, and ducked back into the side room from which he had come.

The hallway had grown chilly because the ambient heat was being sucked out by the twin figures that were now taking form not twenty feet away. From what Lucas had told her, they were using the energy to appear in this world. Della had never believed in such things before. Now she had no choice but to believe.

Why was she seeing things as they truly were

only at the end of her life? She seemed rooted to the floor. All her nerves screamed at her to get up and run away, flee down the stairs, find the front door and run wailing into the street, but she couldn't move a muscle.

Lucas could. The cold white glow of the figures shone on his face to reveal a mask of terror, but he was still able to move. He had seen such things before. While they might have horrified him, they did not destroy his sense of reality.

He stumbled to his feet and yanked Della to hers.

Just then the door at the end of the hall opened.

The wizard stood in the doorway, hands upraised, fingers splayed. He wore black, and only his face and hands were visible through the transparent figures, the disembodied parts glowing in their pale light.

He shouted something in Latin. Della couldn't catch it, but she noted the tone of command.

The glowing figures resolved themselves into images of Ebenezer and Cordelia King. They gazed at Della and Lucas with expressionless eyes.

The wizard shouted again. Ebenezer turned to him, and the wizard shouted a third time.

The two figures glided down the hallway toward them, as silent as death.

"Run!" Lucas shouted.

For once, Della was in complete agreement.

They raced down the stairs, stumbling and nearly falling in the dark. As they got to the bottom, their way was dimly lit by an ethereal white glow. Della glanced over her shoulder and saw the two spirits gliding down to them, picking up speed.

Lucas tugged at her arm. "Come on! We have to save Autumn and Montague!"

Montague.

Hearing the bookseller's name triggered a memory. She reached into her shirt and pulled out the amulet he had given her. It had been tucked under her scarf and the neckline of her shirt, and the goons who had taken her other things had missed it.

The spirits were almost on them now. She gripped it in her hand and turned to Lucas.

"How do I make this work?"

"How should I know? Clutching it like a security blanket sounds like a reasonable plan."

Della remembered what Richard had said to Ebenezer's shade in the cemetery.

The spirits were almost on them now.

Suppressing her fear and summoning her will,

she thrust the amulet in their direction, opening her hand so they could see it, and shouted, "Begone! Begone! Three times I tell you, begone!"

They paused. Their expressionless faces fixed on the amulet dangling from her fingers.

Della hesitated, unsure what to do next. Richard had said something else, something that might have been medieval Latin mixed with some other language. She couldn't remember that gibberish to save her life.

Literally.

Lucas and Della began to slowly back away, not daring to turn around and leave the ghosts behind them. After the first few steps, Ebenezer and Cordelia slowly moved forward, keeping their distance but not letting their prey get any more ahead.

Footsteps on the stairs. The wizard's shadowy figure appeared behind the ghosts.

"Forward!" he shouted in Latin.

The two shades surged at Della and Lucas.

"Stop!" Della shouted, clutching the amulet. She put as much force into her will as she did her voice.

The spirits hesitated once more, barely an arm's length away.

A low growl emerged from the wizard's throat.

He stepped forward, stopping just behind Cordelia, her small ethereal frame illuminating his face from below. He glared at Della and *pushed*.

It wasn't a physical push. He was too far to reach with his corporeal body. Instead he pushed with his mind.

Della felt it in her chest, like an iron fist pressing against her heart.

And she felt it in her spirit. She felt herself cringe and curl up. She felt the urge to turn away and hide, like she had turned away and hidden for so much of her life.

The ghosts began to inch forward, and Della shivered and gripped the amulet. They were almost on her.

Della wavered. Weakened. She was fighting a battle she didn't know how to fight. This wasn't fencing or a test of intellect. Her struggle with these spirits was on a totally different level.

The spirits closed in. Cordelia's image waved before her, and in the corner of her vision, she saw Lucas drawing back before Ebenezer.

Della trembled. The charm Montague had given her was failing. Or more likely, she was failing. She didn't know what to do. Perhaps she lacked the strength.

All the old doubts came back. She had never been the strong one, never been able to stand up for herself. Hiding behind books and science had been an illusion. Now faced with danger, she wasn't up to the challenge. Della sobbed.

She forced herself to face Cordelia. With the last of her will, she looked into those milky eyes.

"I know you don't want to do this," she said in a tremulous voice. "I know you're being forced to be a part of this. First by your husband and then by this evil man at the end of the hall. I don't want any part of this either. We don't have to fight. We're the same. We're both victims."

Cordelia's face puckered a little, as if trying to hear Della's words from a great distance, as if Della was calling across a giant rift. Then understanding dawned on her face.

And she laughed. It was a silent, mocking laugh. Della did not need to hear anything from her long-dead throat to hear the condescension in her reaction.

Cordelia's face twisted in bloodlust, and her claw-like hands reached for Della's throat.

Della went rigid as the ghost's fingers clenched around her neck like a cold iron band, cutting off her breath.

She struggled, trying to tear the ghost's hands away. Her hands passed through and felt not tangible flesh but only frigid air. The only solid feeling was the pressure against her windpipe.

Della's head felt like it was going to explode. Her knees buckled, and the small figure of the dead girl smiled mockingly.

And Della understood. This was no victim, no underage bride forced to join in dark rituals. Cordelia might have been that at first, but her soul soon twisted so that she enjoyed the rites, enjoyed the power they gave her. Something had probably been stained in her soul even before Ebenezer married her. Perhaps he had seen it, and that was why he had chosen her.

But the wife had soon become the master. Her power was the greater one. Her cruelty was the more deeply rooted.

Della had been tricked by appearances, and she was going to die for her ignorance.

Dimly she could hear Lucas shouting something, some incantation. Whatever it was, it wasn't doing any good. She could barely hear it over the cackling of the man who had summoned these shades and the throbbing in her own ears.

The dim hallway grew dimmer. Della felt herself

weaken. She knew she only had a few more moments of consciousness. After that, darkness.

And then what? Death? Or eternal servitude as some enslaved spirit?

No. She hadn't come so far in life only to be some plaything for the creep who owned this place.

With the last of her strength, she focused on the icy fingers cutting off her air. She pictured them weakening, loosening, pulling back.

The pressure on her neck lightened. She still couldn't breathe, and the world was fading fast now, but she had seen a glimmer of hope.

Della redoubled her effort, imagining Cordelia being thrown back. For an instant, the grip ended, and she managed to let out the spent air in her lungs. Desperately she sucked in fresh air, but the fingers clamped down on her once more, and she was left with nothing.

It was over. Her last attempt had failed. The world had faded almost entirely now.

She grunted and fell to the side as the grip was torn from her throat.

For a minute, she lay helpless and gasping on the floor, unable to see what was going on. She saw a swirl of white and heard two men shouting, then she felt strong hands pull her up.

The world spun. She tried to steady herself. Focus. Lucas had her and was pulling her back toward the staircase. In the middle of the hallway, the two spirits were entangled in a struggle, their images merging into one another to appear as a twisting white tornado. The bald man at the end of the hallway was screaming commands that were going entirely unnoticed. His assistant, the one who had attacked them with a machete, peeked out of the side door, his startled face glowing in the white of the apparitions.

"We've got to go!" Lucas shouted, dragging her to the stairs.

Della stumbled, her body still weak. She gripped the railing with one hand and clung to Lucas's neck with the other. Lucas led her down into darkness.

"Can barely see a thing," Lucas grumbled. "I think I remember the way, though."

"What happened?" Della gasped.

"Ebenezer attacked Cordelia."

"Why?" That didn't make any sense.

"I don't know. We have to get back to the others."

The darkness at the bottom of the flight of stairs was nearly absolute. They had no time to find a window and pull back the curtains. From up above, they could still hear their captor shouting some incantation and could still see a faint white glimmer from the spirits. Whatever happened in the fight between those two ghosts, Della knew that someone, spirit or human, would be coming after them soon.

She felt stronger now and was able to stand on her own two feet. They felt their way to the next staircase and descended then moved by feel to the cellar stairs.

There, they paused. They could hear rough voices below. The plumbers. The two of them had regained consciousness. Della squinted as a light appeared in the hallway below. It looked like someone's cell phone, turned on farther down the hallway, perhaps near where the men had originally been overcome.

"Who turned out the bloody lights?" a voice shouted.

"I don't know. Hey, beanpole, get back in that room!"

There was the brief sound of a struggle followed by a thud and a slamming door and the click of a lock.

"Let's get upstairs."

Della and Lucas backed around the corner as the light grew brighter and heavy footsteps thundered up the stairs.

They exchanged glances. The two men coming up at them were stronger, tougher, and more aggressive. The last time Della and Lucas fought them, they only won because they surprised them and had weapons. This time they had nothing in their hands.

But they did have surprise.

Della lifted her hands and made a pushing motion. Lucas nodded.

The footsteps drew close. The glow of the phone grew bright.

Della launched herself around the corner. Half a second later, Lucas followed.

They had timed it perfectly. The two plumbers were at the topmost step and froze for that crucial moment, and their two former prisoners rushed around the corner and gave them each a hard shove.

The burly men tumbled head over heels back down the stairs. The phone one of them held clattered down a few steps to land face up, its light still going.

Della and Lucas rushed down after them, Lucas pausing long enough to grab the phone for light.

The plumbers lay at the bottom of the stairs. One was knocked out. The second lay on the floor, gritting his teeth and clutching his leg, which was bent at an unnatural angle.

"You bastards!" he bellowed as Della and Lucas ran past.

"Look who's talking," Della grumbled.

They rushed to the door and found the key still in the lock. They turned it and opened the door and found Montague just beyond, standing there terrified. Autumn lay on the bed, still shackled. Her haggard face lit up.

"You came back! Did you find the keys?"

Della's stomach turned. "Um, no. But we have one of their phones. Let's call the police."

Lucas glanced at the screen. "Bloody hell. No signal. We have to get upstairs."

A loud wail echoed from above.

"Upstairs might not be a good idea," Della said.

Montague pointed down the hallway. "The garage is just down that way. We can get out through there."

"Now it makes sense," Della said. "This house is built on a slope, with only the garage opening out to the surface. Let's go."

"But what about me?" Autumn wailed.

They all paused. Another shout came from above. The man with the broken leg bellowed, "They're down here!"

Della looked at the staircase then back at

Autumn and then back at the staircase. The man still lay there, clutching his leg, but now he gave her a wicked, hungry grin.

They needed to get out now. Autumn rattled the handcuffs and sobbed.

20

IT WAS the hardest decision Lucas had ever had to make. His friend lay bloody and helpless on the bed, and he had to leave her. If they stayed, they'd probably all be recaptured or worse. If they left, they could call the police. Help would be on its way within a few minutes.

"We'll be back," he said.

The look Autumn gave him cut into his heart.

"This way," Montague urged, stumbling ahead of them. He was still groggy from the gas but managed to make good speed.

Not as hard for you, is it? Lucas thought.

They rushed to the door at the end of the hallway, using the plumber's phone for light. The door led to the large concrete garage where they had been before. The van took up much of it. Della and Lucas went to the garage door and pulled it open. Montague looked in the van.

"My keys and phone are here."

"Are there keys in the ignition?" Lucas asked.

"No."

"What about our stuff?" Della asked.

"I don't see it."

The garage door rattled open.

"No time to look," Lucas said. "Let's get out into the street and make the call."

The phone was already showing a signal. Lucas dialed 999 as they ran down the long, curving driveway to an iron gate. It, like the fence around the property, was topped with iron spikes, the typical protection of wealthy residents against London's large population of burglars. Lucas wondered how the gate opened.

Suddenly the lights came back on in the house, illuminating their path.

"Idiots," Della said, "They did that just in time." She rushed to a button they could now see set back from the gate and hit it. The gate slowly opened.

The emergency services answered, and as Lucas ran with his friends through the gate, he breathlessly made up a story of seeing a woman being dragged into the house.

"What is the location?" the operator asked.

Lucas glanced at the number on the gate. "Number ten."

"Number ten what?" the operator asked. She sounded a bit exasperated.

Lucas glanced around and cursed under his breath. He did not see a street sign.

"What is the road, sir?" the operator asked again.

"Millstone Drive!" Montague said, getting onto Google Maps in record time.

"Number ten Millstone Drive," Lucas said. "Please hurry. I can hear her screaming in there."

"A patrol car is on its way and should be there in less than five minutes."

Lucas turned to his friends. "It's over."

"We can't stay," Montague said.

"What do you mean?" Della demanded. "The police will take it from here."

"No, I didn't get a chance to tell you. I've figured out the spell they are working. It's too far advanced to stop on its own. Even if they don't do the final ritual, the spirits will be released."

"What spirits?" Lucas asked.

"Spirits of dead usurpers. They're trying to overthrow the monarchy!"

"What do you mean?"

"They're hitting power points all over London, using illegitimate and unrecognized royal blood. While you were out about town, I found the ritual. It's a ritual of weakening. I also scanned through crime reports of the Metropolitan Police and found they've conducted human sacrifices on several points."

"Then they could kill Autumn at any moment!" Lucas moved toward the mansion, but Montague restrained him.

"Not yet. Listen! They have more power points to hit to complete the ritual. For that, they need living royal blood. They have to keep Autumn alive until the final ritual. The previous human sacrifices were just normal people, used to open the flows of power. It's her blood that actually makes the spell work. But if they don't complete the ritual, those flows of power remain open. Spirits will break through to our side and cause all sorts of havoc."

Della put her hands to her throat. She had twice almost been killed by a ghost.

Montague went on. "Let the police come and

arrest these people. They'll save Autumn. But we have to make tracks. If we're here when the coppers arrive, they'll take us in for questioning. It won't be long before they recognize our faces from the papers, and then we'll be under arrest. We won't be able to close the power lines, and who knows how many will die!"

A siren wailed in the distance, coming closer. Montague glanced in that direction and put his hands on Lucas's shoulders.

"We have got to run. I'll explain further once we're out of danger. Not canceling the ritual will be almost as bad as if they finished it. Come on!"

Still Lucas hesitated. He glanced at Della and saw the doubt in her face as well. Montague's was the only face that had been recognizable in the press photos. He had the most to lose. The book dealer hadn't exactly shown a lot of courage in this affair. Was he lying to save his own skin?

The siren drew closer. A fainter one, also headed in their direction, joined the first.

Lucas looked around. All the houses here had gates and fences. There was nowhere to hide.

Montague tugged at Lucas's arm. "Come on! We've already called the police. There's nothing more we can do for her."

The house lights were on, but no one had emerged. What were they doing in there?

Montague moved a few steps away and made an urgent gesture for them to follow. "Come on!"

Lucas studied the man in front of him. He was not brave, that was true, but he was also not a back-stabber. Montague didn't have to help, and yet he had broken into Highgate Cemetery and the Red Lion pub, risking himself to help Autumn. He couldn't have done all that only to lie now.

Could he?

What Montague said made sense, from what little Lucas knew about magic. A bungled ritual done by someone with power but not ability could be more dangerous than one done properly, and that guy back in the house had obviously not been able to control those ghosts he had summoned. Ebenezer had actually attacked Cordelia. His gut told him to trust Montague, that there were bigger forces at work here, and calling the emergency services was simply not enough.

But to leave Autumn...

"We should go," Della said.

That decided it. She sounded like she spoke out of impulse, and her impulses had proven right time and again.

They ran down the street in the opposite direction of the approaching sirens.

Just as they were rounding the corner at the far end of the block, a police car appeared at the opposite end of the street. Lucas, Della, and Montague paused, half hidden by a postbox.

The van shot out of the garage, heading for the gate. Just before it made it, the patrol car cut off the exit. The van swerved and slammed into the brick post by the side of the gate. Two officers leapt out of the patrol car, drawing Tasers. A second patrol car roared around the far corner of the street.

"Job done," Montague said. "Let's go."

Lucas felt a bit better now. While it still seemed an awful thing to do, the police had control of the situation and would take care of things. Autumn would be brought to a hospital, and her kidnappers would be brought to justice. He wondered what she'd say to the authorities. That officer Della had spoken to would have some explaining to do to his chief. He had dismissed the possibility that she had been kidnapped and been fooled by her message for help, and now here she was handcuffed in a cellar. Lucas hoped that officer would lose his job.

They hurried through the residential neighborhood until it opened out into a busier shopping district. From there, they caught a night bus that brought them into central London, switched to another bus heading for Bloomsbury, and an hour later walked into the comfortable familiarity of Bedford Square.

They had a surprise waiting for them.

As they entered the square, they saw a patrol car parked outside Montague's house.

"Bloody hell," the book dealer muttered. "Did they spot me or something?"

They hid behind the fenced park that took up the center of the square, peering through the greenery.

Della squinted. "Hey, isn't that Richard?"

Two officers flanked a black man standing in front of Montague's house. In the poor light, with the man's back turned, it was hard to make out, but it did indeed look like Richard.

"He picked a bad time to show up," Lucas said. "Do you think they recognized his face in the paper?"

Montague shook his head. "Couldn't have. I wouldn't have myself. No, there's been problems with junkies hopping the fence and shooting up in the park. They probably think he's one of them."

"Well, go tell them that you know him," Della said.

"Me?" Montague said, putting a hand on his chest. "With my face in every tabloid in London?"

"Give me your keys," Lucas said.

"Why?"

"Hurry up before they cart him off."

Montague handed him the keys, and Lucas walked around the fenced-in green space, coming into view. He could see the detained man was indeed his friend Richard. The police glanced at him and turned back to their suspect.

Oh, so you see a nicely dressed white man, and you don't give him a second thought?

Lucas walked up to the officers, who finally paid attention to him.

"This is my house. Is there a problem?" he asked.

Richard thankfully kept a poker face.

"You live here?" one of the officers asked.

"Yes. My name is Montague James. This man is my friend."

"I'm sorry, Mr. James, but we had a complaint from one of the neighbors that this fellow was lurking around the area."

"Knocking at a door does not constitute lurking," Richard said. He looked angry. He also looked bleary eyed and listless. Lucas wondered what was wrong with him.

Then the officer asked Lucas what he least wanted to hear.

"Do you have any identification on you, sir?"

"I don't have my wallet on me, no, but I do have my house keys. Look."

He walked up the steps and opened the front door with a flourish.

The officers nodded. "All right, sir. It's just that this man appeared under the influence."

"I have the flu," Richard said. "I told you."

"This is a known location for drug addicts. We've had many complaints."

Lucas noticed that the officer did not address Richard as "sir."

Richard's eyes sparked with anger. "Want to search me?"

The officer cocked his head. "Do you consent to a search?" He sounded surprised.

"Only if you apologize once you don't find anything."

"How about you just show me what's in your pockets, eh?"

Richard slapped the book about German royalty down on the hood of the police car with a thump. A bag filled with toiletries and some of Della's clothes already sat on the hood. Briefly Lucas wondered what excuse Richard had made up for carrying a bunch of women's things. With deliberate, showy movements, Richard turned out his pockets to reveal keys, a wallet, and nothing else.

The officer took the wallet and rifled through it, finding nothing of note. After a minute, he handed Richard back his possessions.

"Do I get my apology now?"

"Have a good evening, sir."

The police climbed back in their patrol vehicle.

"*Do I get my apology now?*"

The patrol car drove off.

"Sorry about that," Lucas said.

Richard's eyes blazed. "You're not the one who needs to apologize."

"Well, you won't get an apology from them."

"Obviously not. Where's everyone else?"

Montague and Della came into sight.

"You all right?" Della asked.

Richard smiled. "Nothing I haven't dealt with before, honey. At least this time I'm not actually high."

"We have much to discuss," Montague said, grabbing the keys from Lucas and hurrying inside with a fearful look over his shoulder.

They went into Montague's reading room.

"Lucas, if you'll stand sentry at the window, I'll brew us all a cup of tea."

"Very well."

Della threw her hands into the air. "We just got free from a band of murderous kidnappers, Autumn may still be in captivity, ghosts are coming out of the woodwork, and you're making *tea*?"

Montague looked at her in wonder. "You're in England, darling."

"*And* everyone keeps cracking jokes."

"Age-old English coping mechanism. Got us through the war and helped us defeat Jerry."

"We have to *do* something!"

"Don't get hysterical. We will do something once we figure out what to do."

Montague went off to the kitchen. As he bustled around with the kettle, he called out to them. "So while you were out in the city and Richard was making his excuses to the NHS, I was getting things done. As I said earlier, I recalled that several unsolved murders had occurred in the past few weeks. While normally I don't pay attention to such things, I only noticed the reports because they all seemed to happen along ley lines or at nexus points. Until Autumn got kidnapped, I didn't pay much mind to it. Now I see a pattern. These were human sacrifices. It's a powerful ritual, second only to royal blood ritual. It helped prime the ley lines to be used for more powerful magic. Once the groundwork was prepared, they kidnapped Autumn to use her blood for the real ritual."

"Which was?" Richard asked, slumping into a chair.

Lucas looked at him with concern. He looked ill.

"To undercut the royal family. The seat of English monarchy has been in London for more than a thousand years. Their power is tied to the ley lines that run through the nation and meet here at the city's various sacred spots. Any taint on the ley lines will weaken them. By using illegitimate and unrecognized royal blood, they are hurting the royal family."

"You mentioned that they will sacrifice Autumn," Della said. "What will that achieve?"

"That's the final ritual. It's sympathetic magic, like a voodoo doll. The previous blood rituals make the ley lines run with the power of her blood. When she is sacrificed, it will send ripples through the ley lines that will have fatal consequences to the royal family."

Fear hit Lucas like a splash of cold water. "They mean to kill the queen?"

"Most likely or the heirs. It's an ingenious form of assassination, far more effective than a bullet because everyone will think the royal, or perhaps more than one of them, died of natural causes. Most likely a heart attack, since the assassins are hurting the heart of the kingdom, its ley lines."

"But why?" Della asked.

"The United Kingdom has no shortage of enemies," Montague said. Lucas could hear the water beginning to boil. "I doubt it's the Islamic terrorists. They wouldn't touch black magic. They will blow themselves up with enthusiasm but dread any hint of the supernatural. Perhaps the Russians or some homebrewed terrorist group. The main thing is that we need to stop them."

Della passed her hand across her face. Lucas saw it was trembling. His were too.

"You mentioned that even if they are all in police custody, what they've started will still go on," she said.

"Yes, in an unfocused way. The taint they've put in the ley lines will undercut the city itself. It will be felt in any number of ways—increased violence, fatal accidents, and the kind of hauntings that nearly killed you and Lucas."

"Has Autumn called you?" Lucas asked.

"It's been less than an hour," Montague said.

"Check your phone."

"Oh, very well." He pulled his phone out of his pocket. "No, she hasn't called. She's more likely to call you."

Lucas groaned. "And my phone is in that wizard's house."

Della's jaw dropped. "So is mine. Along with our wallets. The police are going to find those."

Montague came out of the kitchen with the tea pot and cups on a tray. "That's serious. But it will take them time to find all that in that big house and more time to track you down. That gives us a chance to put this thing to rest."

"How?" Lucas asked, taking a cup.

"We'll have to do purification rituals at all the key points where there was a sacrifice. I still need to research how to do that. I didn't have time before those goons jimmied the lock and hauled me away."

"First we need to call the police and find out if Autumn has really been freed," Lucas said.

"We're all wanted," Montague said.

"Look, all three of us filed the missing person

report," Lucas said, trying to control his impatience. "Della and I can't call because our phones will be found in the kidnapper's home, if they haven't been already. That's going to lead to a lot of questions I'm not prepared to answer at the moment. You have to call. They know your face, and they know your name, but they haven't connected the two."

"And I don't want to give them the chance, dear boy," Montague said, taking a sip from his tea.

"We have to make sure she's all right."

"I don't see how they could have escaped with her. You saw the police head them off."

"Just make the damn call!" Della snapped.

Montague called the police, identified himself, and asked about Autumn. He waited for a time then hung up with a shrug.

"I told you it's too soon. They said they have no record of her missing since the original case was dismissed. I'll call back in half an hour."

Lucas stood. "I'm going back to that house and see what I can find out from the police."

"I'm coming with you," Della said. "Montague, we'll need some money and your transport card."

"Very well," he said, handing them his Oyster card and forty pounds. "In the meantime, we need to research this ritual more thoroughly. Richard, you're the most knowledgeable of this lot. You can help."

Richard nodded slowly. He looked half asleep.

Montague's brow furrowed. "What's wrong with you, anyway? Have you been smoking cannabis?"

"I took some herbs that raised my temperature to fool the nurse at my local clinic. The trouble is they've made me weak. Basically, I feel like I have the flu."

"Well, at least you're not contagious," Montague said.

"How long are you going to be like this?" Lucas asked.

"Just a day."

Montague slapped him on the back. "You look well enough to go through some books with me. Just don't smoke in the library, eh?"

Richard's brow furrowed. "When have you ever seen me smoke in a library?"

"Oh, I didn't mean cigarettes. I meant ganja, mon, the sweet herb." Montague said this last bit with a fake Jamaican accent.

The bookseller headed off to the back room, where most of the rarest volumes were kept. Della watched him go, clearly appalled.

"Why do you tolerate that?" she whispered to Richard.

"Tolerate what?"

"What do you mean? He's always pointing out you're black and gay. He's so rude about it!"

Richard laughed. "Oh, honey. Being black and gay in England's poshest postcode, I've heard a lot ruder comments than that!"

"But don't all his microaggressions bother you?"

Richard rolled his eyes. "No, because I'm not a micro-person. I'm a little more worried about the police and this ritual that's brewing. Let's get to work."

"Sounds like an excellent idea," Lucas said, heading out the door with Della. "Richard, barricade this door. They already broke in once, and we don't know if anyone from the gang might still be free."

"I'll be sure to. Perhaps I'll use Montague."

"Sounds like another excellent idea."

Lucas and Della hurried out into the night.

21

SEVERAL PATROL CARS were still outside the mansion where they had been held. Police tape had been strung across the open gate, and the van stood where they had last seen it, smashed against one of the brick pillars to one side of the entrance.

The front door to the house was open, and the lights were all on. From their position on the far end of the street, Della and Lucas could see figures moving about in the windows.

Several of the neighbors stood on their front steps, watching the drama unfold.

Della approached the nearest one, a plump middle-aged man in a purple silk bathrobe.

"What's going on?" she asked.

"Not really sure. I go to bed early, and the sirens

woke me up. By the time I took a look outside, that van had been in a wreck, and the police were hauling away three fellows. They gave the police quite a time. One fellow punched an officer and didn't stop until he got Tased." The man chuckled, obviously entertained by the scene.

"Then what?"

The man shrugged. "Then nothing. The police have been searching the house. I suppose it's drugs. It usually is in cases like this, isn't it? No neighborhood is respectable in this city anymore."

"They only arrested three? Are you sure?"

The man looked at her oddly. "That's all I saw."

"What about the woman in the house?"

"What woman? What do you know about it?"

"Huh? Oh, I'm... staying with the Andersons down the street. I chatted with a woman who was staying there just yesterday."

"Oh." The man turned back to the crime scene.

Della let out a breath of relief. She was so bad at lying. Good thing it looked like the English didn't know their neighbors any more than the Americans did.

She walked back to Lucas. "I'm going to talk with the police."

"I'll go."

"No, it's better if I do. Police suspect women less than men."

Before Lucas could object further, she squared her shoulders and walked over to three police officers standing next to the gate. Della adjusted the scarf around her neck to make sure none of her bruises showed. That would cause some awkward questions.

As she approached, a female officer stepped away from the other two and blocked her way.

"Nothing to see here, ma'am." Her tone was dismissive.

"Oh, I live on this street, and I was wondering if the woman living here was all right."

"Woman?"

Della gave a description of Autumn. The officer shook her head.

"There's no one matching that description here."

Della ground her teeth and tried to keep from grabbing the officer and screaming the whole story in her face.

"Oh, I met her earlier this evening. She said her name was Autumn Birgit Saxe-Coburg. There was some middle-aged man all in black with a shaved head with her. He was acting very hostile. Didn't want to speak to me at all. He seemed to get angry that she was speaking to me and grabbed her wrist and pulled her inside."

The officer was writing in her pad now. "And when was this?"

"Earlier tonight, around nine."

"Did you catch the man's name?"

"No, he didn't talk to me at all. He just sort of... glared. Autumn looked like she was scared of him."

The officer asked for more details of their clothing and appearance. While this was going on, Della noticed a fourth officer searching the van. He came out with some clear plastic evidence bags. In one of them she recognized her phone.

"Found these in the glove box," he said to the other police officers.

Damn, why didn't I take the time to look there?

Because you were scared out of your mind and running for your life. That's why.

Just then her phone lit up and started buzzing. Della jerked.

The female officer noticed her reaction and turned to look at the phone. Della could see the name on the screen.

Sebastian. Her ex-boyfriend.

Perfect timing.

The officer turned back to her. And stared.

Della realized she was sweating. She could feel her eyes bugging and her jaw clenching. She knew she looked as guilty as hell, and she couldn't do a thing about it.

Think. Think.

"It was very upsetting," she said, her voice hoarse. "He was so... sinister. I'm sure she was being abused."

The phone kept ringing. The policeman holding the bag opened the Ziploc seal and pulled it out.

"We'll be sure to look into it," the female police officer said, her face relaxing. Obviously she had felt a surge of suspicion and then dismissed it when faced by what to all appearances was only a nervous witness.

Then the officer made Della so frightened that the persistent buzzing of the phone faded into the background.

"Could you give me your name and contact details? Just in case we have any more questions."

"Hello?" the officer with her phone said. Pause. "This is Special Constable Ianson speaking. Who is this?" Pause. "This phone was found at a crime scene."

"Excuse me?" the female officer said, waving a hand in front of Della's face.

"Oh, sorry. I... um... my name is Mary. Um, Mary Gardiner."

"And your phone number?"

"Oh, I'm a tourist. I don't have a British phone."

"No, your friend Della isn't here. Who's this?"

"Where are you staying?"

"Um, the Hotel Russell. Room 315."

The officer wrote that down in her pad.

"I see. Well, here's my card. If you think of anything else, even the smallest detail, please call us."

"Right, um, I'll do that."

Della snatched the card and was about to beat a hasty retreat when the officer said, "We'll call you at your hotel if we hear anything."

"Right. Thanks."

Della glanced at the other officer, the one with her phone, but he had already hung up. She turned stiffly and walked away, feeling like every movement betrayed her guilt.

"What happened?" Lucas asked when she returned to where he was standing.

"They found our phones. Sebastian, of all people, just called me."

Lucas frowned. "What the devil does he want?"

"I don't know. I didn't exactly grab the phone from the cop's hand and ask. Does it matter?"

"I suppose not," Lucas said, although he kept frowning.

They started walking away.

"That was a close one," Della said, letting out a great gust of air. "I suck at lying. They didn't find Autumn or the wizard. I don't think they found that shrimp with the machete either."

Lucas rubbed his temples. Suddenly he looked very tired. "Let's get back to Montague and Richard," he said. "Perhaps they've figured something out."

"Let's call first. See if they have anything we need to chase up. There's a phone box over there," Della said, pointing at the corner of a larger street where the neighborhood shifted from residential to commercial.

Entering the bright-red phone box, they ignored the colorful postcards offering Thai massages and spanking sessions and called Montague's number. The scantily clad women gave them come-hither looks as Montague's phone rang.

"Pity he isn't here," Lucas murmured, looking at the walls. "He'd have something pithy and marginally inappropriate to say about all these ladies."

Della shook her head. Did the English have to joke about everything? Then she remembered Montague calling it a coping mechanism, a bit like her hiding and reading. More useful than turning into a hermit, though. You could still get things done. It all sounded a bit ridiculous, though.

Montague picked up, and they told them what they had learned. Della pressed her ear close so she could hear his reaction.

"That's bad. Here, I'll put Richard on. He's had sleep and still managed to discover something important."

Richard's voice came on the line.

"I went through that book Della bought. Buying it was a premonition to be sure. It mentions the ancient line of Anhalt and some legends we haven't found anywhere else. One of them traces the line all the way back to the Celts. The Anhalt line at that time originally lived along the northwest coast of Germany, just west of the Jutland peninsula, not in central Germany where it is today. They were a mercantile tribe, trading along the coast and as far as England. They secured an alliance with the Iceni Celtic tribe in England through several royal marriages. That makes them related to Boudica."

Della blinked. Boudica was a Celtic queen who

led an uprising against Roman rule in 60 AD. The Celts managed to burn several Roman towns and forts before finally being defeated. She focused on Richard's next words.

"Montague and I think the final ritual will be at her traditional burial place. Boudica was a rebel, her burial place is along a ley line, and she is of royal blood related to the Anhalt line. Della, if you're listening, I want you to understand that your intuition is probably your most powerful asset. You plucked this book out from among thousands, and it had the exact information we need."

Lucas moved over a couple of inches so Della could speak into the phone.

"You said you haven't found this legend anywhere else. How do you know it's true?"

"The connection with the Anhalt line is too important to be a coincidence."

"But why are they doing this?"

"I'm not sure. Like we talked about before, it could be any number of groups. Whoever that fellow who captured you is, he's done his homework. Doesn't seem to be powerful enough to handle what he's doing. There's no shortage of egomaniacs in this business. The important thing is that we now know where the final ritual will be."

Della's mouth went dry. She swallowed and asked, "Where?"

"King's Cross station between platforms nine and ten."

Della blinked. "Come again?"

"Before that area got built up, a village called Battle Bridge stood there. There was a ford across the River Fleet there. Local folklore said that this was where Boudica and her Iceni lost the battle against the Romans. Boudica is said to be buried on the spot. It happens to be a nexus of the ley lines as well, including one of the lines where the water weird attacked you."

Della's skepticism kicked in. "Is there any archaeological evidence for this?"

"Have they found Boudica's body? No. And the area has been built up too much for too long to do any real excavations. The village and the ford are definitely attested in the historical record, and it has been proven that the area has been inhabited since at least Roman times. There was a military camp guarding the ford."

Della glanced at Lucas and nodded. She remembered reading how Boudica came down from the north, slaughtering Romans and burning their camps as she and her huge army advanced. The Iceni burned Verulamium, and that was only twenty-five miles north of Londinium. The Roman capital, just two days' march away, would have been their next logical objective.

And that military camp by the ford blocking access to the city from the north would have been the logical place to stop them.

"All right, what do we do? You've convinced me."

"Really?"

She had never heard Richard sound so surprised.

"Not really, but yeah. I don't know what's going on anymore. So are you saying that bald guy and his little creep are going to kill Autumn at King's Cross station?"

"Most likely, yes."

"How in the world do they expect to get away with it?" Lucas asked.

"Who knows?" Richard said. "Perhaps they don't care if they avoid the police or not. Once the ritual is finished, all hell will break loose. They might be able to summon a lot worse spirits than Ebenezer and Cordelia."

Della touched the scarf around her neck. She had barely survived those two. The second time, it had been Ebenezer who saved her.

That still didn't make sense to her.

"So when will this happen?" Della asked.

Montague's voice came back on the line. "Any midnight will do, as it's a time of transition, and they are attempting to disrupt one status quo and replace it with another. But we believe they aren't quite done. There's one more nexus point associated with the Anhalt line here in London where there has been no murder or ritual that we know of. Lucas, are you familiar with the Steelyard?"

"Yes, but it hasn't existed for almost two centuries," Lucas said.

"Come now, you should know better than that. It's a nexus point, and that's where they'll be doing a blood ritual, most likely at two o'clock this morning. The planets make an especially good alignment at that time. Mars and Saturn, the god of war and the king of the gods. Most appropriate."

"Two o'clock?" Lucas glanced at his watch. "That's half an hour from now."

Della hadn't realized it had become so late. Her fatigue from earlier had vanished in the adrenaline rush.

"You can make it if you take a taxi," Montague said. "I've already called Cassandra to meet you there."

Della's heart sank to hear that woman was going to be back on the scene. She forced herself to speak.

"Shouldn't we call the police?"

"And tell them what?" Montague asked. "You don't have to confront them. All you have to do is disrupt the ritual. Stop them from speaking the right words or defiling the ley line with royal blood."

Della hadn't thought of the Steelyard as a possible location for one of the rituals, but now that Montague and Richard had mentioned it, the place made sense. She had read about it once in a book on medieval history, back in her undergraduate years when she was thinking of being a medievalist rather than an archaeologist studying prehistory.

The Steelyard had been the location of a trading post for the Hanseatic League since the thirteenth century. A group of merchants from the North and Baltic Seas, it had included many Germans among its members. While Montague and Richard hadn't had time to explain, no doubt they had found evidence that the Anhalt family had ties to the Hanseatic League.

This wasn't surprising. While royal families tended to look down their noses at commerce, the Anhalt was a minor line in need of cash. Its extended relations would have been encouraged to get into the trading game to make some much-needed money.

And it certainly worked for several centuries. The Hanseatic League was one of the first great merchant associations. Its members had connections across northern Europe and were the first to introduce the idea of checks to the Western world. A slip of paper for, say, a hundred guilders written out in Amsterdam would be honored in Riga hundreds of miles away. The league controlled most of the northern trade for much of the Middle Ages and the Renaissance via local trading houses called kontors. The Steelyard was London's kontor and was so powerful that these German-speaking merchants had better trading rights and lower taxes than native English merchants.

That caused a lot of friction, but the kontor was powerful enough to run much of London's trade until Queen Elizabeth suppressed the trading colony in 1598. It was only then that England had a chance to be a power in its own right and eventually become an empire.

The head merchants of the Hanseatic League had chosen their location well. Her companions explained that it stood on the eastern edge of the old Roman and medieval city on a ley line running through Bishopsgate, one of the old city walls, now vanished. Della could see a double meaning in picking this spot. It would symbolically undercut the city's finances, with London being the financial heart of the nation, and it would also reassert foreign control over the nation, a control that had been rescinded by a queen named Elizabeth.

I'm beginning to think like these people, Della thought with regret. *What kind of world am I being sucked into?*

As Della sat in the back of a taxi with Lucas as the driver took them to the location, her mind reeled. There were so many layers to this spell, so many ways that it would hurt the monarchy and the nation itself. It had to be some sort of foreign group. Yet that wizard had a London accent. Well, it wouldn't be the first time someone had sold out his nation for power.

The problem was that this guy looked like he was trying to do more than he was able. That made him even more dangerous because it made the results of his spells unpredictable.

"So what's there now?" Della asked.

"Cannon Street station. A major Tube station. It's all quite built up."

"I bet there's another river there."

"What?"

"Just a feeling."

Suddenly Lucas snapped his fingers. "My god, there is! The Walbrook flows near there to empty into the Thames. It's buried just like the River Fleet."

Della leaned back in her seat.

"Great." She sighed. "That's just great."

She wondered if she had the strength to fight another water spirit like the one that nearly killed them all beneath St. Bride's Church.

22

THE TAXI DROPPED THEM OFF, according to Lucas's instructions, a block from Cannon Street station. Cassandra was standing there waiting, looking a little nervous in the nearly empty street. It was late, and the City, being a business district, did not have much of a night life. In the distance, a group of drunken men in business suits staggered away from them, howling at the night like a pack of wolves, their voices echoing off the high-rises. A police siren blared in the distance. Otherwise no one was about.

"We're going to stick out like sore thumbs," Lucas said by way of greeting. "How are we going to sneak up on them?"

"We have to find them first, darling," Cassandra

said, taking his hand. Lucas pulled it away and glanced at Della.

"Let's go," Della grumbled.

They started to walk toward the station. Lucas recounted everything that had happened to them. Cassandra turned pale.

"Remarkable. And you say Ebenezer saved you from Cordelia?"

Della nodded. "I sensed that she was the more powerful of the two. If we'd hung around, I bet she would have beaten him and come after us." She turned to Lucas. "Do you think she was the one really in charge? It was her handwriting on the documents, remember. Montague assumed that she was acting as a secretary. What if she was the master and Ebenezer the slave?"

"But Ebenezer was the one to make the rounds in occult circles," Lucas said. "He was who led the rituals. We have documentation for that."

Della shrugged. "Maybe he was only a front man. It was the nineteenth century, after all. Women didn't have much of a place, and she wouldn't have been taken as seriously as he was."

"I think your little American might be right, Lucas. It would explain why she was trying to give her river water instead of holy water. She tried it twice. That's pretty foul stuff in both places, made fouler by the magic cast there. It would have made Della sick, maybe even worked to put her under Cordelia's control."

"Why target her?" Lucas asked.

"Because she has more Talent than you and less experience," Cassandra said.

"Is that an insult or a backhanded compliment?" Lucas asked.

"Can we stop the English nattering and focus on what the hell we're going to do about the murderous cult lurking somewhere in this neighborhood?" Della grumbled.

Lucas smiled. "Americans. Always wanting to do something first and talk later."

They came within sight of Cannon Street station, at the base of a glass-and-steel office building that was brightly lit even at this late hour. The last Tube had stopped running half an hour before, and no one was about except for a bored-looking security guard standing out front.

Cassandra walked up to him, putting on a smile that she had once reserved only for Lucas. The guard suddenly stopped looking bored. No doubt his heart had started racing. Lucas could see him stand a little taller and move his hands to make sure his shirt wasn't wrinkled. Lucas had done the same thing when he saw Cassandra, once upon a time.

"Excuse me, have you seen my uncle? I'm looking for him. Bald? Wearing all black?"

"Yes, he just went down Steelyard Passage a couple of minutes ago with some other bloke."

The security guard pointed at the far corner of the building, a block away.

"Oh, thank you. My auntie wasn't with them?" Cassandra asked.

"No, just your uncle and his friend." The security guard paused, glanced at Lucas, and then back at Cassandra. Lucas could almost hear the wheels turning in the guard's mind as he tried to figure out an excuse to ask for her phone number. In the end, he only said, "Have a good night, and if you need anything else, feel free to ask."

He smiled awkwardly. The three of them walked away.

"So what's the plan?" Della asked.

Lucas grimaced. "I don't really have one, I'm afraid. I was hoping they'd bring Autumn and we could stop all this right now."

"Where could they be keeping her?" Cassandra wondered.

No one had an answer to that. Lucas's heart beat

faster as they approached Steelyard Passage, a narrow street running between Cannon Street station and another large building.

They stopped in their tracks as a dark figure peeked out from around the corner and quickly withdrew.

"Damn it. Spotted," Lucas said.

"Come on," Della urged. "Let's stop this now."

She sounded determined, angry. Her whole world had been torn apart, and Lucas could tell that all she wanted was for this to be over. She'd do whatever it took to make that happen.

They ran toward the entrance to the side street, angling away at the last minute so as not to come around the corner and into any sort of trap. Instead, they ended up in the middle of the street, well away from the corner, and looking down Steelyard Passage.

What they saw made their hearts clench with terror.

They had come right in the middle of the ritual. They were almost too late.

A couple of feet back from the entrance into Steelyard Passage, a narrow street dwarfed by the tall buildings to either side, stood the small, slim man who had attacked them before. He gripped a machete, uncaring that he had a CCTV camera right above him. Lucas figured him for a Londoner, someone who knew that in this dead neighborhood after the pubs and Tube had closed, no one would be monitoring the cameras. He was chanting quietly in a strange tongue Lucas did not recognize. A few steps behind him, the wizard was chanting the same alien words.

The wizard faced Cannon Street station. Complex designs had been drawn in chalk on the ground, and the wizard was just raising a gleaming gold chalice above his head.

Lucas had seen many rituals before but nothing that felt this dark, nothing that carried such a gut-wrenching signal of imminent evil.

It was the boldness of the act that most affected Lucas. Here these two men were, brandishing weapons and raising chalices that no doubt held the blood of his friend, right in the heart of the down-town financial district.

There was confidence in their actions—and arrogance. The wizard and his weaselly little accomplice knew they only had to complete two more rituals for the royal house of the United Kingdom to come crashing down.

They only had to complete this ritual, and then

they only had to kill Autumn, and it would all be over.

Cassandra started her own chant. Lucas recognized it as a spell of negation and could feel a ripple of power emanate from his ex-girlfriend. The two men standing in Steelyard Passage raised their voices in response.

Lucas hesitated, unsure what to do. Cassandra was an adept occultist, but she was facing a powerful, multipart royal blood ritual that was nearly complete. She might be able to slow them, but she would not be able to stop them on the spiritual plane.

And with that man standing with a machete between them and the blood ritual, they couldn't stop them on the physical plane either.

Della took a more mundane course of action. She rushed over to some nearby construction and grabbed two traffic cones. Hurrying back, she launched one of the heavy rubber cones straight into the machete man's face.

Lucas took that as his cue. He leapt forward and punched him before he could recover.

He had it timed perfectly. Almost. The man was just bringing up his machete, and Lucas only managed a glancing blow on his cheek before having to jump back to avoid getting his hand cut off.

Then Della got to work with the other traffic cone. Holding the tapered end, she swung it, connecting with the harder base. The man grunted but did not fall.

Before he could raise his machete again and cut Della down, Lucas leaped in again and gave him a better punch this time.

The man backpedaled, flourishing his machete. Della and Lucas should have pressed him, but the sight of that keen blade made them hesitate just for a moment.

A moment was enough.

The wizard shouted a final note and poured a dark-red liquid onto the arcane designs on the pavement.

Lucas felt a sickening lurch as a taint ran through the ley line at their feet.

The wizard turned and grinned at them in triumph, shaking the golden chalice mockingly.

Lucas groaned. They had failed.

But those two weren't done with them yet.

The smaller man let out a yell and charged them with the machete.

They had no choice but to run, right out into the street, dodging a black cab that sped by, the driver and his passenger appearing as brief startled stares in the passing windows, and then they continued back up the street from which they came.

Back toward Cannon Street station, where the security guard was already on his radio.

The machete man spotted him, too, turned tail, and ran.

"He's calling the cops," Cassandra said. "Come with me to my car. It's not far."

"They'll track us via CCTV," Della objected. "They'll get your plate number."

Cassandra shook her head. "They'll do that already. I'm already recorded parking my car and joining you. I must say, Lucas, you picked a hell of a way to have a reunion."

They hurried two blocks to where Cassandra's car was parked, hopped in, and sped away. It wasn't until they were halfway to Montague's house that Lucas felt like he could breathe again.

"Lucas, darling," Cassandra said as she drove through the nearly empty streets. "While I'm perfectly happy helping you save the monarchy, I don't fancy getting arrested. I can't go all the way back to Montague's. His picture is in all the papers. It will link me with him, and considering that the police are no doubt looking for us as we speak, it will do neither me nor Montague any good. Shall I drop you off at a bus stop?"

"Yes, I suppose you should. We'll meet tomorrow morning to plan. We have to stop them at King's Cross at midnight tomorrow, or it's all over."

"Today, Lucas," Cassandra said. "It's half two in the morning."

"Right," Lucas grumbled. "We have less and less time and keep losing ground."

"Rest," she said. "All of you get some rest, and we'll plan in the morning like you said. Della, you must hate having to stay in that musty old house with such a creepy fellow as Montague. Care to stay at my flat? You can change when we go visit them in the morning."

"All right," Della said.

Lucas looked at her with a mixture of surprise and worry. Those two, chatting away together over breakfast? Who knew what they'd get up to?

You have bigger worries than that, Lucas reminded himself.

Nevertheless, when Cassandra dropped him off at a bus stop and pulled away with Della, he got the strange feeling that when he saw the two of them again, everything would be different.

He waited for some time before the night bus

came and nodded off once or twice on the trip back to Bloomsbury. It was well past three when he entered Bedford Square. He was so tired, so preoccupied with the events of the night, he didn't see the police officers coming for him until it was too late to run.

The officers flanked him, barking at him to put his hands in the air. He did as he was told, his heart sinking. One pulled out a pair of handcuffs, turned him around, and ordered him to put his hands behind his back. Across the square, the door to Montague's house was open, and Richard was being led out by another officer.

Lucas hung his head, staring at the ground as he felt the cold steel clamp around his wrists.

"I'm sorry, Autumn," he whispered.

LUCAS AND RICHARD sat slumped in the police station office. Before them, glowering at the unhappy pair from behind a desk, was an old acquaintance.

Detective Chief Inspector Matthews.

A trim man in his late thirties, Lucas and Richard had faced him in similar circumstances a couple of times earlier that summer.

"Well, well, well, it's so nice to see you again," the police officer said. "It's not often I get to come down to London. Refreshing to visit the big city, isn't it? I've come on a bad night. Seems the whole city decided to misbehave. The local force doesn't even have a spare officer to question you. That's fine, because I'm happy to perform the service. Now, may I ask what you two gentlemen are doing here?"

Lucas and Richard exchanged glances. Silence seemed to be the best option.

DCI Matthews raised his fingers one by one. "Criminal trespass into Highgate Cemetery. Breaking and entering. Destruction of property. Affray. Running from the police…"

"Officer," Lucas began. "We didn't have—"

"And obstructing the course of justice. That's what I'll add to the charges if I think the next words out of your mouth are a lie."

Lucas paused. "How did you find us?"

DCI Matthews laughed.

"You two aren't nearly as clever as you think you are. All summer I've been monitoring a continuing case here in London. Several unsolved murders at the nexus points of ley lines."

Lucas looked at him in shock. Had those words just come from a policeman's lips?

DCI Matthews smiled and nodded. "Yes, just the kind of tosh you're into, isn't it? And how do I know about it? Because some clever chap on the force here discovered the connection. His hobby is London folklore. No, don't look at me like that. He isn't some self-styled wizard. He's an amateur historian. Always boring the chaps with obscure trivia. Well, for once, his pub-quiz knowledge came in handy. After our little chats a couple of months ago, I just knew you two would pop up in the middle of it. When I saw the newspaper pictures, I knew I was right."

Lucas blinked. "Newspaper pictures?"

"The ones showing the two of you breaking into Highgate Cemetery and The Red Lion pub. Oh, your faces aren't visible, but I know it was you. And we've identified Mr. James. We'll be picking him up shortly, I'm sure."

So Montague was still free? Well, that was some good news at least.

But what could Montague do? He lacked the courage to face their enemy.

DCI Matthews fixed them with a hard stare. "Who is that woman you were with?"

Lucas bit his lip. So Della was still free as well. Good.

"I'm waiting," the police officer said.

"Midnight tonight. King's Cross station. Either platform nine or ten," Lucas said.

"I beg your pardon?"

"That's where you'll find the murderers."

"Do explain."

And so Lucas and Richard explained. It was the only way to stop the ritual now. The police would never let them go, and they were sure to round up the others sooner rather than later. It was over. The police would have to handle this if they could. If they believed them.

DCI Matthews listened to the entire story without comment. When Lucas and Richard had told it all, when their words trailed off to an uncomfortable silence, the police officer sat and stared at them for a time.

Then he shook his head.

"Two healthy, educated, well-off chaps like you... what the devil are you doing mixed up in all this? Why can't you do something useful with your lives?"

"It's my faith," Richard said.

"Blood rituals and raising the dead? That's your faith?"

"That's what we're trying to stop," Lucas interjected.

"Oh yes, you're the good wizards. Wearing all white like Gandalf while trying to sneak into Mordor."

"Frodo," Richard said.

"I beg your pardon?"

"Gandalf didn't sneak into Mordor. Frodo did," Richard said.

Lucas winced. His friend had a terrible habit of talking back to policemen. He really needed to speak to Richard about that some time.

DCI Matthews glared. "Pardon me for not being as well versed as you in fantasy worlds."

"All this is true," Lucas said.

"The part about the kidnapping and blood ritual certainly is," DCI Matthews said, raising Lucas's hopes. "The rest of this is enough to put you in the lunatic asylum."

"We need to intercept them at King's Cross," Richard insisted. "A woman's life is in danger."

DCI Matthews sighed and rubbed his eyes. He looked tired and fed up.

"No, *we* don't need to intercept them. My fellow officers and I do. And we will. We already have your friend's photo on file for a number of harassment offenses against the palace. Give us a complete description of the two suspects in her kidnapping. We'll round them up."

"We really need to go along," Lucas said. "There are forces at work—"

DCI Matthews slammed his hand down on the desk, making Lucas and Richard jump in their seats. An officer who had been standing guard outside the door opened it and looked inside, a question on his face. DCI Matthews waved him off. Then he fixed them with a cold stare.

"Give me their descriptions. Now."

Lucas and Richard did as they were told, adding every detail they could think of about what the two kidnappers might do next. DCI Matthews listened with a mixture of exasperation and attentiveness.

"Ley lines and royal blood sacrifice?" he muttered as he took notes. "What's wrong with Anglicanism? Church not good enough for you?"

When they were finally done, Lucas summoned the courage to ask what would be done with them.

"You're in a cell until all this is over. I have enough charges to hold you, along with suspicion of kidnapping."

"Kidnapping!" Lucas and Richard said at the same time.

"We know you're involved in this case, and you

have shown no definite proof that you're not involved in the kidnapping."

Before they could sputter a reply, DCI Matthews summoned in the officer from the hall and had them led away.

It was a long, morose wait in the jail cells for them. They paced. They tried to sleep and kept getting awoken by shouts in the hallway as a steady stream of other prisoners was hauled in. They ran through the events they'd been through over and over again and could come up with no better plan than to hope the police would manage on their own.

A very, very slim hope.

Then they got company.

The first was a drunk, brought in around ten in the morning. What surprised Lucas was how respectable he looked—business suit, well-groomed. Having lived in England all his life, Lucas was accustomed to respectable-looking people having too much to drink and misbehaving in public—one could almost call it a national pastime—but not at ten o'clock in the morning.

The police let him in and closed the cell door behind him, and the drunk staggered over to a spare bed and flopped down.

"I can't believe I did that," he muttered.

Lucas and Richard ignored him, lost in their own worries.

"I mean, I like a drink or two every now and then," the drunk went on, "but this morning I woke up, saw the whiskey in the cabinet, and drained the whole thing! Why did I do that?"

The man's voice trailed off.

"Why did I do that?" he repeated. A few minutes later he was snoring.

Half an hour later they got another cellmate.

In stark contrast to the first, this was a young tough with a shaved head, impressive muscles, and an Arsenal Football Club tattoo on his neck. He had the flattened nose and numerous facial scars of someone who enjoyed getting into fights. Lucas knew the type and was frankly afraid of them. It was their kind that was responsible for so much of the violent crime on London's streets.

But it was the young thug who looked frightened.

He sat on the edge of his bunk, one leg jacking up and down, fists clenched, and kept looking around him with darting glances. At first, Lucas wondered if he was high, but after watching him for a while out of the corner of his eye, he realized that he was terrified.

"You all right?" Lucas asked after several minutes.

The man shook his head violently but did not reply.

After a few minutes, he let it spill out.

"You know what they banged me up for?"

"No, what?" Richard asked.

"Firing my Glock in my flat."

Lucas tensed. The last thing he needed was to be locked up with a gang member.

The youth must have seen his expression because he said, "I don't shoot anyone or nothing, just keep it for home defense, like. And to get respect. Gotta have respect in my neighborhood."

"So what were you shooting at?" While Lucas normally wouldn't talk to this kind of person, the man's behavior had made him curious.

His eyes went wide. "A ghost."

That got their attention. The man went on.

"There was this old lady living in the next flat. Been the witch of the neighborhood for years. Always yelling at us when we were kids for having a kick about in the foyer or drinking in the park. Right pain in the arse, she was. She knew I was selling, just a bit on the side to help out at the end of the month before we got the dole. Nothing big. Should have minded her own business. I wasn't bothering her. She was always knocking at my door at all hours and screaming at me.

"Well, last month she died. Heart attack. Probably from screaming all the time. Serves her right. Then this morning I'm sitting there watching the telly and eating some cereal when there's a loud knock on the door. *Thump, thump, thump,* like she always used to do. I open up, worried it's the coppers, and there she is! I swear to God it was. Nearly had a heart attack myself. And then she came in. Sort of drifted in the air. And she was screaming at me, her mouth all moving a hundred miles an hour like always, but I could hear no words."

"You sure it was a ghost?" Richard said.

"Yeah! She's been dead for a month, like. I saw them cart her body away myself. Her flat's already been given over to someone else. When I saw her drifting at me like that and screaming without making a sound, I panicked. I grabbed my gun and emptied on her. The bullets just passed right through and into the hallway. Then I blacked out. When I woke up, the coppers were already cuffing me."

Lucas and Richard exchanged glances.

"What? You don't believe me."

"Actually, we do," Richard said. "We saw some ghosts yesterday too."

The young man swore and curled up on his bunk.

Richard moved over beside Lucas. "Even if the police do stop this fellow from killing Autumn, we're still stuck with the ley lines tainted and all sorts of trouble," he whispered. "This is only the beginning."

Lucas didn't have an answer for that. He could only hope that Cassandra and Montague would stay free long enough to do something about it. It looked like he was out of this fight now.

He was wrong.

Almost twenty-four hours after he had been put in the jail cell, DCI Matthews entered to take him out of it.

"It's eleven o'clock. Your mate is supposed to show at King's Cross in an hour. You're coming with us."

"I'll help in any way I can, sir," Lucas said.

Richard stood. "I'd be happy to help too."

DCI Matthews jabbed a finger at Lucas. "Him, not you."

"Why?" Richard demanded. Lucas gritted his teeth. Now wasn't the time for a confrontation.

"Because he doesn't have a police record, and you do. Come on, Mr. Lancaster."

"But, Officer," Lucas objected. "He has more magical talent than I do. He'll know better how to break—"

"Move it, before I change my mind!"

Lucas sighed and did as he was told.

23

WHILE LUCAS and Richard were stewing in the jail cell, Della had spent a short night sleeping like a stone on Cassandra's couch before her hostess woke her.

"There's trouble," Cassandra said, her hair flattened on one side from the pillow and her eyes still puffy from sleep. Della felt annoyed that despite this, Lucas's ex-girlfriend still looked gorgeous.

"What's the matter?" Della mumbled, looking at the window and seeing it was still early morning.

"Montague called. Lucas and Richard were arrested last night."

She sat bolt upright. "What?"

"The police caught Lucas as he was coming back to Montague's house. Richard was arrested inside.

Montague got away because he went to an all-night chemist to get some medicine for Richard. He's still feeling unwell from the herbs he took. It was pure luck Montague didn't get nabbed as well. When he saw what was happening, he went across town and stayed at a hotel for the night."

"And he didn't bother calling us until now?"

Cassandra shrugged. "He may be well read, but he isn't the smartest chap you'll meet. Besides, he's scared silly. Sillier than usual. He daren't return to his house. He's coming over here, and we're going to figure out what to do."

Della groaned and rubbed her eyes. She could use another twelve hours of sleep, but the main thing was to save Autumn. It was up to them now.

And Cassandra and Montague didn't exactly make the best allies.

Then another thought struck her.

Why was she here? She didn't like Cassandra, didn't feel comfortable spending time with her, but when she offered her living room as a place to sleep, Della had immediately agreed.

Somehow she had felt a premonition that there'd be trouble at Montague's place.

Della didn't know how her gut feeling had told her the police were about to pounce, only that she was glad she had trusted it. She hadn't even consciously had the thought. It was just that when Cassandra offered her couch, Della had immediately felt relieved and accepted the offer. She hadn't even questioned why she would agree to spend time with Cassandra.

Della made a mental note to rely on her instincts more often. If she had been more sensitive to them, Richard and Lucas might still be free.

By the time Montague made it over, Della had washed up and drunk some of the mud water the English called coffee. It tasted terrible, but at least it woke her up.

Montague looked worse than she felt. He didn't look like he had slept a wink all night. His hands trembled, and he kept looking around the room as if ghosts or policemen were going to jump out from behind the furniture. Considering how the last few days had gone, Della couldn't really blame him.

"We have to call the police and tell them what's going to happen at King's Cross," Della said.

"I already have," Montague said, gratefully accepting a cup of strong tea from Cassandra. "I called anonymously from a phone box. Lucas and Richard might have told them as well. But that will solve only part of the problem."

Della nodded. They needed to purify the ley lines, or there would be all sorts of trouble. She would have never even considered this a possibility a week ago. Now she had to face facts.

The day was spent going with Cassandra to all the spots Montague told them had been scenes of blood rituals. The two occultists had designed a ritual that would help purify the ley lines, lessening the effect of the dark ritual. It wouldn't break the spell, but it would weaken its power and hopefully give them an edge that evening.

"We can't solve the problem completely until the people who stopped the ritual are thwarted," Montague warned. "As long as their personal power is invested in the ritual, it still goes forward."

So they went all over London in Cassandra's car —to crossroads of modern streets that ran along the same paths as old Roman roads, to historic churches built atop pagan groves, and to the courses of ancient rivers now hidden under the modern city. At all of them, they performed a brief ceremony, Cassandra chanting in low tones while Della focused her energy, picturing pure-white light, as Montague had instructed her to. At the end of each ceremony, Cassandra poured a small amount of water

Montague had done something to onto the pavement.

It felt ridiculous, and Della's social anxiety disorder kicked into high gear any time they did it. She kept her eyes closed, desperately trying to focus on her part of the ceremony as she flushed from embarrassment at the comments made by passersby.

"Use the Force, Luke!" bellowed someone with a Cockney accent.

An American woman whispered, "Oh, look, Harold, it's some British custom. Take a picture."

And yet despite the acute embarrassment and the snickering and the cutting comments, Della could feel a change taking place. At each spot, she felt a taint, a low unsettling of her stomach, as if she had just sipped some spoiled milk. That lessened with each ritual.

It didn't stop her from grabbing Cassandra's hand and rushing away from the staring crowd after each ritual was complete. She found herself shaking on each trip to a new spot, having to force herself to go through it all again.

Cassandra didn't help. She never said anything, but the disparaging looks she gave Della showed that she didn't think much of her as a spiritual warrior.

The worst was when they returned to the crypt of St. Bride's. The young minister recognized her and came over to ask how she was doing. She felt tempted to tell him that she felt terrible, that she was in a spiritual battle like nothing he had prepared for in his seminary, but instead she just smiled and said she was fine. Then they shook him off and went to the crypt.

She was horrified to see the Roman tiles were cracked in two places side by side, like someone had been standing on them. She had a sneaking suspicion she knew who that someone was. A large sign had been added, warning against climbing the barrier.

Great, I just wrecked a piece of Roman London. Some archaeologist I turned out to be.

They performed the ritual. It only took a minute, which was just as well because just as they finished, the minister came storming down.

"What are you doing?" he demanded.

"A blessing for the church," Cassandra said with surprising honesty, giving him a sweet smile.

The minister was impressed neither by her honesty nor her smile.

"What's that you poured on the tiles? Those are ancient artifacts! Part of the church's history!"

"Blessed water," she said, edging past him to head for the stairs. Della followed.

"You," the minister said, jabbing a finger at Della. "You were here the day the tiles got broken. Did you climb the barrier and stand on them, or one of those two men you were with?"

Della stopped, guilt rooting her to the spot. The minster frowned at her. Cassandra grabbed Della's hand and yanked her toward the stairs.

"I'm calling the police!" the minister shouted. "I have your faces on CCTV!"

They sprinted out of the church and wove through the thick downtown crowd the two blocks to Cassandra's car, the Englishwoman laughing all the while.

"What's so funny?" Della panted as they finally got into the car.

"Wasn't that fun? Didn't you see the look on that man's face?"

Cassandra started the car, and they pulled away.

"Fun? I might have been responsible for breaking those tiles, and then we went and poured water on them and thumbed our noses at a minister!"

"Oh, live a little!"

"What a disgusting world you people live in," Della snapped.

Cassandra frowned, and Della flinched, startled.

It was the first time the woman had betrayed her true emotions.

"Don't lump all occultists in with that lot. Would you like me to lump you in with the Ku Klux Klan just because you're American?"

Della raised her hands. "All right, sorry. It's just that if you start down this kind of path, it's easy to get corrupted. We just poured water mixed with who-knows-what onto a priceless archaeological treasure. Tonight we're going to commit criminal trespass. Again. A lot of people wouldn't consider it much of a jump from there to stealing. And from stealing they could end up doing worse. A lot worse."

Cassandra sighed. "True enough. You know why Montague's business is so popular? You can find many of the books he sells in libraries, but those copies get stolen or have pages cut out. That even happens at the national libraries such as the British Library and the Bodleian. Many of the people following this spiritual path are attracted to it because of dreams of personal power. This makes them selfish and can lead to temptation. It happens in more mainstream faiths, too, although the effects aren't so, shall we say, *sinister*."

"Lucas isn't like that," Della said, remembering how Cassandra had called him selfish.

"No, his problem is more deeply rooted. He's selfish because he lost so much at a young age. It's not his fault, but it makes getting close to him difficult."

"Who says I want anything more than friendship?"

Cassandra chuckled. "Silly girl."

Della gritted her teeth. She hated being condescended to, especially because she could never come up with a witty comeback.

In all these rituals and their crisscross journey across the city, Montague did not come with them. Instead, he stayed in Cassandra's apartment, watching television.

"I'm wanted by the police, dearie," he had said that morning when Della complained. "And being seven feet tall and weighing only eighty kilos, I do stand out a bit."

While that was true enough, Della knew it wasn't the real reason. He was scared. Well, so was she, and she was out there getting it done.

They came back to Cassandra's place exhausted. Montague was still in front of the television. Both of them tried to take a nap to prepare for the final struggle that night. Try as Della might, sleep escaped her. She suspected Cassandra was the same.

DELLA COULD NOT BELIEVE she was doing this again. She, Cassandra, and Montague sloshed through knee-deep water in a storm drain under King's Cross. The place stank, and the passing trains overhead made an ominous rumble. The headlamps on their yellow hard hats revealed nothing, but the place didn't feel right.

Della had been pleasantly surprised when Montague volunteered to come. He was shaking when he told them.

"You're going into danger, and you'll need a man to protect you."

For once, Della thought of a cutting comeback right off the cuff. In fact, she thought of several. She kept quiet, though. They did need his help, even if he wasn't the knight in shining armor he thought himself to be.

He certainly wasn't acting like a knight in shining armor now.

"How do you know where you're going?" Montague asked, bending over almost double to avoid bashing his head against the low roof and looking around nervously. "All these drains look the same. Are you sure we aren't lost?"

"I've been down here before," Cassandra said. "Besides, see those numbers painted on the walls? They're codes we use at Thames Water. I know exactly where I am."

"Why would you come down here?" Della asked, trying to keep her voice down, as every noise echoed in the confined space. "I thought you were a senior engineer or something. Lucas said you work in an office most of the time."

"I've cast some spells down here, trying to commune with Boudica's spirit."

Della groaned. Talking with dead Celtic queens? She couldn't decide whether she objected to the idea because it was ridiculous or because it was possible.

"Did the spells work?" Montague asked.

"My Talent doesn't really extend in that direction. I did get some sensations, though. This is definitely the site of the old battlefield, and she is certainly buried on or near this spot."

Della felt the old cynicism rise in her. She quickly suppressed it. She was exploring a new world now, and she had to keep an open mind.

If only these people didn't believe any quack historical theory that came along, it would be easier to deal with, Della thought.

Except that far too many of those quack theories

are turning out to be true. Have I just wasted the last five years of coursework?

They came to a fork in the tunnel. The channel continued straight ahead, and to either side, other tunnels sloped up. Della's headlamp revealed that they leveled out after a time, giving access to a higher level of tunnels. Cassandra paused.

"Have you gotten us lost?" Montague asked.

Della looked at her face. No, she hadn't gotten them lost. Cassandra was terrified.

A moment later Della realized why.

A slow feeling of dread crept over her. She looked around, trying to locate the source, but couldn't. Montague paled, feeling it too.

"What is that?" Della whispered.

"The ritual," Cassandra replied. "It's nearly done. We're close."

"It's not midnight yet." It couldn't have been later than 11:45, and the ritual wasn't even supposed to start until midnight. They had entered the tunnel system with plenty of time to spare.

The water rippled.

And yet it did not ripple. It made no sound, and Della did not quite see its movement. It was more as if she imagined the water rippling, moving forward as if being pushed by a large body farther down the tunnel.

The ripples continued—imagined or seen with something other than her sight—and Della's heart sped with fear, for she knew this was not imagination.

"Wh-wha?" Montague stuttered.

They all looked down the tunnel ahead of them. The ripples grew stronger and came with increasing frequency. A series of pale-white lights appeared at the limit of their beams and drew closer to resolve themselves into a crowd of silent, charging figures.

Charging at them.

"This way!" Cassandra shouted, pointing up the ramp to their left.

They scrambled up the ramp, slipping and sliding on concrete made slick from water and mold. As they made it to the top and found themselves in an access tunnel even smaller than the drain they had left, Della felt a shuddering chill that forced her to turn around.

At the bottom of the sloping drain stood a horde of ghostly figures. To normal sight, they were indistinct, hazy, and little more than mist. Yet in her mind's eye, Della could see them more clearly.

A group of men in furs and skins, wielding

spears and swords and rectangular wooden shields. And in front of them, a raven-haired woman with a sword in her hand and fury on her face.

No. A deposed queen, looking for vengeance. For two thousand years, she had lain below the city while others ruled in her rightful place. And now she had been summoned with a royal's blood to depose what she saw as a false monarch and a false dynasty.

And when the final act of the ritual was consecrated with the death of the monarch's distant relation, it would give the spirits the power to wreak havoc on the nation.

The ghostly horde rushed up the slope at them, as silent as the tomb they promised.

Once again Della, Cassandra, and Montague ran, Montague frantically pointing the way.

"I can feel it!" he shouted. "The nexus is just down this tunnel."

The tunnel's air was fresher here, and Della noted grills in the ceiling through which she could see light several feet above.

"We must be right beneath the platform," she said.

"They're going to get in and do it here," Montague said, glancing over his shoulder at the pursuing figures. "It will be out of sight of the police and closer to Boudica's grave. Come on!"

But they were slowed by the cramped space, their heavy rubber waders, and their fear. The ghostly army began to catch up.

A low boom rumbled through the tunnel.

"That wasn't a train. What was that?" Della cried.

Smoke puffed through the series of grilles in the ceiling.

"They've set off a distraction!" Cassandra said. "They must know the way down here from the platform. They're using the smoke to hide their movements."

Della cursed. Even if Lucas and Richard had managed to convince to police to come, they wouldn't be able to find the men holding Autumn.

The smoke began to fill the tunnel, making them blink and cough. The ghostly army was almost upon them now.

Montague stopped. He looked first at Cassandra and then at Della.

"I'll hold them. Find Autumn and stop the ritual."

Della glanced at the ghostly figures. They were

only a few yards behind, raising their weapons. "But—"

Montague shoved her. "Go!"

The bookseller turned to face Boudica and her Iceni army, raising his hands and beginning a chant.

Cassandra grabbed Della's hand, and they ran, Montague's echoing chant following them down the tunnel.

"Come on. He won't be able to hold them for long," Cassandra said. "I think it's right up here."

After about twenty meters, they came to another intersection. Cassandra paused just enough to read the numbers spray-painted on the wall and ducked right.

Just as they did so, they heard a scream from behind them.

Della stopped, but Cassandra pulled her on.

Still coughing from the smoke that hung in the passageway, Della wiped her eyes and saw lights ahead. They immediately turned off their own and found that a faint light filtered in from the grates on the ceiling. They could see the cold white glare of flashlights shining from around a corner. Voices echoed to them, but they could not make out the words.

A chill ran through them. Della didn't know

whether it was from the ritual ahead or the ghostly army behind. Either way, they didn't have much time.

Even so, they moved carefully, remembering how they failed the last time they foolishly rushed in. Trying to make as little noise as possible in their waders, they crept up to the corner. As they did, they could hear a woman whimpering and two men chanting. Della's heart trembled. They were getting ready to sacrifice Autumn.

Cassandra leaned in close and in an almost inaudible whisper said, "When we round the corner, focus all your energy on the wizard. Imagine shutting him down, breaking his power. It will stop the ritual."

"How's that supposed to work?" Della whispered back.

Cassandra looked worried. "It doesn't. Not without years of intense training."

From the way she said it, it didn't sound like Cassandra had had "years of intense training" either.

No time for doubt. We need to try it.

But as they rounded the corner and saw Autumn lying handcuffed a few meters away at the feet of the two kidnappers, they discovered they didn't have the chance.

Because between them and the ritual stood the shades of Ebenezer and Cordelia King.

Della took a step back. The ghosts were looking right at them. She reached into her shirt and pulled out the amulet Montague had given her.

The bald wizard turned and shouted something in Latin. He gripped a long, thin steel knife. His little assistant wielded a machete.

The ghosts glided toward them. Cassandra started chanting. Ebenezer and Cordelia hesitated. With a force of will Della could feel, Cordelia pushed toward them. Ebenezer hung back as the wizard berated him, splaying out his hand and screaming arcane words that seemed to lash at the male spirit.

Cordelia looked over her shoulder and shouted something at her husband that the barrier between life and death made silent to Della's ears. She splayed out her hand at him in the same gesture as the wizard, and Ebenezer moved forward, reluctance on his ugly face.

And suddenly Della understood.

It had been Cordelia all along. Ebenezer had power but nothing compared to Cordelia, neither during their lifetimes nor after they had passed to the other side. He had always been a front man, a tool for an evil young woman to get what she wanted in a male-dominated society. Because no matter what her spiritual power, she was still shackled by the customs of the early nineteenth century.

Ebenezer might not have been a model citizen, but he was now a victim, just as much of an unwilling tool as the sobbing Autumn lying on the hard concrete.

Except, unlike Autumn, he was not powerless.

Della made the boldest decision of her life and charged right at the two ghosts.

Cordelia lashed out at her as she passed, a cold spike of pain cutting through Della's body as Cordelia's claw-like hand passed through her.

Della stumbled but broke through her grip and reached out for Ebenezer.

There was no body to touch, so Della focused on the image of grabbing him, and together they launched at the wizard and his accomplice.

The little machete-wielding assistant was in front. His face turned to a mask of terror as Ebenezer enveloped him.

His scream was cut short by the ghostly hands encircling his throat. The machete clattered to the concrete floor, to be scooped up by Della.

A glance over her shoulder told her that

Cassandra was struggling with the female spirit in a battle Della didn't understand and could probably not be of much help in.

Looking back at the wizard, she saw she had her own battle to fight.

The man stalked toward her, his keen knife at the ready.

"You picked the wrong girl to challenge to a fencing match," she said, getting into stance and readying the machete.

The wizard snorted and swung at her.

Della parried his knife, the steel striking steel to make an echoing clang in the confined concrete tunnel. She sliced at his leg, but the wizard nimbly jumped back. Della pressed her advantage, going again for his leg—she could not quite stomach aiming for his head—and the wizard parried her blow.

This wasn't going as well as she'd hoped. The machete was too short and too heavy, not like the light and finely balanced epee she was accustomed to. Plus, this guy was surprisingly quick.

The wizard darted forward, feinting to the left and slashing out to the right. Della spotted the move, but the machete was so slow that she almost didn't parry in time. Before she could counterattack, he had ducked out of reach.

A cry from behind distracted her. She resisted the urge to look. Instead she attacked again. The wizard parried once, twice, then tried to strike back only to have Della dodge to the side and slam down on his lighter blade with enough force to put him off balance.

She struck again, harder this time, looping the blade around in a quick circle to make the knife fly out of his hand to ricochet off the wall.

Della put the machete up to his throat.

"Surrender."

He only grinned.

A cold, tight grip clenched around her throat and forced her to her knees.

Cordelia stood above her. Cassandra lay a few meters away, groaning and barely conscious.

"We might as well have two sacrifices tonight," the wizard said, picking up his knife.

A white form shot into view and enveloped the wizard. Ebenezer. The wizard struggled, lashing out, trying to utter a spell but unable to speak as he got choked by long-dead hands.

Della struggled with her own ghost. Her pulse pounded in her temples, and her sight dimmed as she tried and failed to release Cordelia's grip.

And then the spirit let go on its own accord, flying to help the man who had summoned her.

Della fell to her hands and knees, gasping for air. Cordelia clawed at her dead husband, pulling him off the wizard.

Calling on the last of her strength, Della surged forward, the amulet in her hand, and screamed into Cordelia's face, "Begone! Begone! Three times I command you, begone!"

The female ghost drifted back, weakened and fading for a moment, then scowled and pushed against Della's will. Della felt it like a slab of ice hitting her chest. She stumbled back, leaning against the wall, trying desperately to fight back. In a flash of panic, Della realized she wasn't strong enough to hold Cordelia off for long. This was a fight she would not win.

She didn't have to. Ebenezer rushed at the wizard, who was just staggering over to retrieve his knife a second time, and plunged his hand through the man's throat.

The effort took all of Ebenezer's energy, and he winked out of existence just as he turned to give a look to Della.

A look of gratitude.

The wizard slumped to the ground, dead.

Cordelia let out a silent scream and faded from view.

Della stood up, stunned. Blearily she looked first at Cassandra, who still lay moaning on the ground, and then at the wizard and his assistant, both dead from Ebenezer's vengeance. Della stumbled over to the wizard, fumbled through his pocket, and found the keys to the handcuffs.

"Thank you," Autumn sniffled as Della went over to release her.

"Stop where you are!"

Della whirled around to see a man wearing an overcoat and holding a flashlight in one hand and a pistol in the other.

That pistol was aimed right at her.

"You're under arrest. What's going on here?"

Della saw a uniformed policeman behind him, and right next to him stood Lucas.

"He's dead," Lucas said. "You've done it! DCI Matthews, this is the man who kidnapped us."

The policeman knelt by the body of the dead wizard.

"I recognize this one. Einhardt Donner. He's an international terrorist and leader of the Nihilistic Front."

"The what?" Lucas asked.

"Radical anarchists," DCI Matthews said. "So radical that most of your garden-variety anarchists think he's a nutter, and that's saying something. Thinks the only way to get a truly free world is to destroy everything and start over. He's wanted in five countries, or was anyway."

"Did you know he was a magical practitioner?" Lucas asked.

DCI Matthews gave Lucas a sharp look. "Yes, but we didn't think it was significant, considering all his other strange ideas. I see now that we missed an important detail."

The words came out as an accusation.

"So wait, this guy didn't even have an ideology?" Lucas asked. "He just did all this to destroy the system and not replace it with anything?"

The policeman gave a bitter smile. "If you think the occult world is dark, try police work."

Della snapped out of her stunned silence.

"Officer, a friend of mine is hurt in the tunnel back there."

She and Cassandra led two police officers farther into the tunnels. The smoke was slowly clearing, but the chill brought on by magic remained. Della could feel it had weakened, and yet there was a lingering sense of it.

"We need to be careful," Cassandra said.

"What happened to your friend?" the officer asked, buttoning up his jacket.

"He was... attacked. We didn't see by whom."

They came to the intersection and rounded the corner.

Montague lay not far off, covered in blood. Several long gashes crisscrossed his body, as if from sword wounds. Just beyond stood the phantom horde, faint but still visible. Boudica stood in front. She raised her sword in silent defiance, and then she and her army faded from existence.

24

ONE WEEK LATER...

Lucas had just got off the phone with Cassandra. One of the down sides of this whole mess was that she now had his new telephone number. She had made several excuses to call.

This time she called to tell him the results of the management's meeting at Thames Water. While she could have been sacked for bringing unauthorized personnel into the company's facilities, the fact that she had helped stop a murder had weighed in her favor.

"I also told them how I was following my faith," she said with a chuckle. "While they gave me one or two odd looks, I think they got worried that sacking me would lead to a religious discrimination lawsuit."

Even so, she was given a reprimand and could not expect a promotion for which she was due. At least she had kept her job.

Her salvation came in the form of DCI Matthews, who visited the board of Thames Water personally to vouch for her help in the case.

As he hung up the phone, he wondered about the police officer. He'd seen more than he had expected, and while he wasn't convinced all this was real, he had turned from an enemy to something approaching an ally. Lucas had the feeling he would be hearing from DCI Matthews again.

His thoughts were interrupted by Aunt Mary walking into the room.

"Was that Della?" she asked.

"No, Cassandra. She managed to keep her job."

"Oh. I hope she doesn't call too much. She was never good for you."

"I know that, Auntie."

"And isolation isn't good for you either. Why don't you call Della? I'll wager she could use a few days in the country."

"When she wants to release stress, she isolates. No doubt she's holed up in her flat, reading obscure archaeology tomes."

Aunt Mary smiled. "Or that neo-antiquarian book Cassandra lent her."

"I doubt it. She'll want to get as far away from all that as possible. She'll read it eventually, though. Her curiosity has been aroused. The only thing stronger than that woman's skepticism is her love of discovery."

"Sounds like you know her well. Perhaps you should ask her to the movies. Give her something normal to do."

Lucas raised a hand. "Please, Auntie, don't try to push us together. Uncle Philip is already pestering me on that front."

"You need to get out more, and from all accounts, so does she."

Lucas rolled his eyes. "I think I've been out quite enough the past few days."

Aunt Mary shook her head, obviously frustrated. "Then go hide in your woodworking shop like Della is hiding among her books."

Lucas smiled. "I plan to. Just like poor Richard, I've been neglecting my paying job." The smile faded. "Auntie, something happened when I was in captivity. I tried to contact you with that technique you mentioned. It was difficult at first, because I didn't know if there was an attendant ritual, and needless to say, I was a bit distracted by my circum-stances, but I think I might have broken through."

That got her attention. She perked up and studied him. "Really? Describe it to me."

"It was... strange. I pictured this house in my mind, and in my mind's eye, I walked through it. I came into the library and looked right at the chair where you always sit. I *saw* you there, and I think you saw me. I could have sworn you looked right at me. Did you sense something?"

Aunt Mary gave a sad smile and shook her head. "No, Lucas. I didn't feel anything. I told you the Talent was passing from me to you. This often happens in families of practitioners. One fades, and another begins to shine. I think you opened a connection, but it was you who needed to complete it."

Lucas raised his hands in an exaggerated shrug. "How?"

"It's a long and difficult process."

From the way she said it, Lucas knew that she doubted his discipline or willingness to go through with it.

Lucas let out a sigh. "I've been avoiding this too long. As you always say, we don't choose this role. It gets chosen for us. I think it's time I accept it.

Perhaps if I had been more diligent, Montague would be alive today."

"Don't blame yourself for that."

"I don't," Lucas said, feeling a little pit of sadness simmering in his heart. "At least not really. But I have to make his death mean something. I need to learn to handle my Talent so that the next time this happens I can stop people from getting hurt."

"That's not always possible in this business."

Lucas slumped. "No, I suppose not. But I can reduce the numbers."

"You seem certain it will happen again."

Lucas nodded, not able to speak.

Aunt Mary gave him a pitying look. "Della would make a good ally."

Lucas gave a wry smile. "It looks like fate has plans for her and me."

"I'm sure it does, Lucas. I'm sure it does."

ON THE OTHER side of town, Della lay in her bed, a warm blanket covering her despite the summer night, two pillows propping up her back, and books scattered all around her. If she had known that her friend was speaking of her over at the farm, she would have laughed to hear how wrong he was. For of all the books on her bed—the archeological journals and the academic textbooks, the fantasy novels and the Latin grammars—it was the book Cassandra had lent her that she was reading.

It fascinated her. It also confused and enraged her. On the surface, all of it sounded like complete nonsense. Pagan rituals surviving into the modern day? Lines of power connecting all of England's sacred sites? Dowsing? Spirits residing in holy wells? Total rubbish, and yet she knew for a fact that some of these things were true. Some of these things had proven deadly.

But only *some* of these things were true. Cassandra, Richard, and even Lucas had said that much of what passed for magic in this world was complete nonsense. So how to separate the wheat from the chaff?

Study. Lots and lots of study. She needed to read as many sources as possible, talk to as many practitioners as possible, and make up her own mind. Lucas had been pushing her to accept this hidden world ever since the fight with her advisor's cult. If she had taken him seriously, they might not have gotten into so much danger. Montague might not have died.

Lucas and Richard had both been deeply affected. While Montague had not been a friend, he had been a mainstay in the occult community for years. And to lose such a prominent member in such a way must have cut deep.

It cut deep into Della's heart, too, more so than she had expected. The man had been arrogant and exasperating, and yet she saw something of herself in him too. He had been a social misfit trying to cover up with intellectualism and the pretense that everything was all right even when it wasn't. She knew what that was like.

And the one time he had reached beyond himself, the one time he had shown true courage, he had been killed.

Della couldn't let that happen to someone else, not if she could help it.

She would need to speak with Aunt Mary. That was the best place to start. Even Montague had been envious of her library. The kindly old woman would guide her to the best books to read.

So she'd stay in her flat for the couple of days it would take to read this introductory book, and once the silence and solitude had recharged her personal batteries, she'd make a call to Lucas and ask to come over.

A smile crept across Della's face. It would be an interesting challenge to delve into that huge library. She'd browsed through it before. Aunt Mary had tomes dating back to the sixteenth century plus many one-of-a-kind manuscripts. It would be nice to sit in that library, working her way through them. It was a quiet, peaceful place filled with knowledge. Hot tea and scones would no doubt be in ready supply, as would stimulating conversation when her eyes grew tired and the words swam on the page. She could be left in peace to read all day, knowing there were kind, sympathetic ears ready to listen in the evenings.

Yeah, that would be nice.

It would be even nicer if Lucas sat right there next to her.

DCI MATTHEWS WAS BACK in his office in the Oxford Central Police Station, but the events down in London still haunted him.

Those figures he had seen.

What had they been? Ghosts? Some sort of delusion? He couldn't be cracking up, could he?

They had looked for all the world like a group of primitive warriors led by a red-haired woman.

Like most Londoners, he had heard the tale that Boudica lay buried under King's Cross. That was a folktale, though, a fun story that had no connection with reality.

And yet he had seen something. The officer with him had seen it, too, and was equally baffled. They had agreed to say nothing to anyone else on the force. For what, really, could they say?

He'd checked the CCTV footage for all over the station and the surrounding neighborhood. There was no way such a large group could have entered the area without being picked up on camera. He checked every camera going back two hours before the sighting. Ran it over and over until his eyes burned—and saw nothing.

But he had seen something. There hadn't just been him and the suspects in that tunnel.

There had been someone else. Some*thing* else.

The police officer passed a trembling hand over his face. He'd seen a lot in his career. Men stabbed to death. Teenagers foaming at the mouth and going into convulsions from drug overdoses. Women beaten to a pulp by savage husbands. But this was something else.

And this wretched case didn't look like it was over. The London police had called him twice now, saying that there had been attempted break-ins at Montague James's house. The first thief was captured and turned out to be some silly occultist. Apparently Mr. James had run a rare book business from his home and had quite the storehouse of rare and expensive nonsense. The second thief had been pursued but had escaped.

Then he received a call from Richard Camilo. That had been unexpected, but DCI Matthews was beginning to expect the unexpected from that joker.

Mr. Camilo had told him he had been contacted by Montague James's attorney with the surprising news that he had been made executor of his estate. Mr. James had no living relatives and wanted Camilo to dispose of the books and disburse the money to various charities.

"There are some powerful tomes and magical artifacts in the house," Richard Camilo said. "I'm going to need some help from the police to protect them."

Fancy that, a convicted criminal asking for help from the police!

But then the man had said something that chilled DCI Matthews to the marrow.

"Lucas told me what happened and what you saw. I think I can rely on you, even if London isn't your jurisdiction. You're in this as much as all of us now."

The police officer had put down the phone and shuddered.

Yes, he was in it now, but Richard Camilo and his friends were mistaken if they thought he was an ally. They flouted the law, breaking into private property, lying to the police, running amok in public places, endangering the lives of others. These people were dangerous.

And the spirits they summoned were even more dangerous.

No. DCI Matthews slammed a fist onto his desk. No spirits. Just a bunch of loonies getting up to no good. He'd show them.

Yes, he'd help Richard Camilo protect Montague James's occult collection, and he would watch him. So these books and artifacts were prized, eh? Well, that made good bait to bring in all sorts of fish.

The occult community was a danger to public safety, and this collection that Mr. Camilo had to offload would be the perfect trap with which to eradicate it.

ABOUT THE AUTHOR

S.A. Beck lives in sunny California. When she's not surfing, knitting, or daydreaming in a hammock, she's writing novels.

www.sabeckbooks.com